INCOMING TIDE

Martha Craig

First published in 2023 by Martha Craig

Publishing services provided by Lumphanan Press
www.lumphananpress.co.uk

Contents

– 1 –

New Boots

Spring 1869

She was up even earlier than usual that morning. After putting on the brown dress that reached to her ankles, Lizzie brushed her chestnut hair and pinned it neatly on top of her head. The other two dresses, hand-me-downs sewn to fit, were in the box.

She picked up the box and glanced over at her two younger sisters, asleep in their double bed, then moved silently in stockinged feet out of the room, down the wooden staircase and into the farmhouse kitchen.

Once she'd cleared last night's ashes from the fireplace, she re-set and lit the fire. Then Lizzie washed her hands at the deep sink, crossed the floor and sat down on a chair against the wall. From beneath the chair she pulled out the new black boots, lifted the hem of her dress, and slowly pulled on and laced up each boot. Putting her feet together, she bent forward to admire them, breathing in the smell of new leather. Until now, boots had been for winter only. For the rest of the year, Lizzie normally went barefoot. Now she had new boots, and it wasn't even winter. There was a movement on the stairs, and she sprang up lightly.

'I'll just set the table, Mam.'

Her mother seemed to have changed towards Lizzie since she had got this, her first, job. Her pawky sayings had always been accompanied by a chuckling laugh. One saying that she had enjoyed repeating was 'Keep your eyes wide open before you marry, and half shut after.' But lately when she had said this, there had been no accompanying laughter.

Later that morning, when Old Tom's cart rumbled into the farmyard, the family gathered to see her off. Lizzie got up on the cart and sat beside Tom. Her father handed her box up to her, and she set it on her knee. As horse and cart moved forward, she turned to wave back to her family, then resolutely faced forward. She knew that with one more backward glance, she could be down off the cart and running back to the warmth and familiarity of all she had known.

The next few miles passed in companionable silence. Tom had been a kindly presence in her life as far back as she could remember. When she had been just a small child, she'd looked forward to his visits to the farm. Sometimes, for a treat, he would lift her onto the seat beside him and take her with him to the other farms he had to visit. Now she sat in that same seat seeing the land open up on either side of the track to display the rich loam of ploughed fields. A haze of green here and there showed the growth of seeds that had been sown earlier. Today, the wide sky was blue, with only a few clouds scattered on the horizon.

'C'mon, Polly,' Tom urged the horse up an incline and then, to Lizzie, 'And do you think you'll like your new job then?'

'Oh aye. My cousin Freda's leaving to get married, so I'll be taking over from her, looking after the bairns mostly.'

'Ah well, you'll know plenty about that.'

Lizzie thought about her two younger sisters and the baby brother who was just learning his first words and began to talk quickly.

'Freda took me to meet the family. They stay in this big house, not far this side of Winfield – but och, you know where the manse is. The minister's a big man but his wife's small and narrow-made.

'There's three bairns. The oldest is Thomas,' she said as she glanced at her companion. 'Same name as yourself, Tom, but he always gets his full name, Thomas. He's nine years old. Next there's the lassie, Christianna, she's four, and then the babby, Mark. D'ye know, Tom, I've never seen such quiet bairns in all my life. The two oldest just sat on the settee and never said a word. Even the babby on his mother's lap was as quiet as quiet could be.' She paused, then added a little smugly, 'Of course, I suppose it's because they're kind of gentry.'

The cart had rumbled along for some time when two figures came into view on the road ahead. As they drew nearer, Lizzie recognised the fishwife and her daughter. The older woman eased the creel on her back as she passed.

'Well, Mrs. Buchan,' Tom greeted her.

'Aye, aye, Tom,' the woman replied.

Behind her, her round-faced daughter stopped and looked up with empty eyes, repeating in a flat voice, 'Aye, aye, Tom.' She looked from Tom to Lizzie and gave a half smile. The woman, who had walked on, called, 'Come away, Dolly. Stop dawdlin'.' The girl dropped her eyes and trudged on behind her mother, holding tightly to what looked like a small bundle of rags.

'They come to our farmhouse,' said Lizzie, 'but they only speak to Mam. The woman won't let the lassie speak to any of the rest of us. And why is she still wearing a pinafore?' she asked, referring to the sleeveless wrap-around the girl was wearing over her dress. 'She's not a bairn. That lassie must be about the same age as myself, about fourteen – or maybe even older.'

'Ah well, you see, Lizzie, the poor lass is just not right in the head,' Tom explained. 'Her mother keeps her close, and maybe the pinafore keeps the boys' eyes off her.'

Lizzie saw the sense of this. A boy wouldn't want to be seen with a girl who was still in a pinafore. She thought then of Donald, with his fair hair and bonny blue eyes. He had come to their farm as often as he could and, knowing he was fond of her, she had grown fond of him in return. Her mother had said of him, 'He seems a fine enough lad, Lizzie, but he just seems to lack *substance*.'

Lizzie had not been sure what her mother had meant, but had a feeling it was tied up somehow with the oft-repeated 'Keep your eyes wide open afore you marry...'

'We're nearly there, then, lass.' Tom's voice broke in on her thoughts. 'Just down this bit of a hill and round the next corner.'

The horse ambled on until it was halted by Tom's 'Woa,

there,' and Lizzie looked to her left. At the top of a slope of rough grass stood the manse. As befitted her new status as a paid working woman, Lizzie got down sedately from the cart and reached up to take her box from Tom.

'Ta-ta then, Tom,' she said cheerily, then walked in her new boots through the gap in the low wall, and on up the path that led to the steps of the front door. As she heard the sounds of the receding horse and cart, she steeled herself again not to turn round. Taking a deep breath, Lizzie lifted the brass knocker and banged it three times on the door.

– 2 –

The Big House

The tiny maid-of-all-work who had let her in had disappeared upstairs to find her mistress, and Lizzie stood in the dim hallway with its smell of beeswax. The only light came from a window at the turn of the stairs. Soon, the mistress of the house came down and, with a sharp beckoning of her finger, rustled ahead of Lizzie into a room at the bottom of the stairs. Lizzie followed her and closed the door. Mrs. Beattie turned her pale face to the girl.

'Well, you know, there's plenty to do in a house with children.' She clasped and unclasped her hands before her as she spoke, then turned abruptly towards the window and repeated slowly, 'Yes, plenty to do.' She paused before turning back to Lizzie and adding briskly, 'So today, you can help Agnes in the kitchen while I take the children for their lessons. Away you go then, away you go.'

She left the room, leaving Lizzie to find her own way along the dim corridor towards what she thought might be the kitchen. There was no-one there, but through the window she could see steam billowing out and up from a washhouse door, where it was snatched and dispersed by the breeze. Lizzie crossed the cobbled space outside, scattering some foraging hens. Inside the washhouse she was engulfed by steam and the strong smell of plain soap. She could just make out the small figure in a white mobcap who was bent over the deep sink, scrubbing clothes against a washboard.

'Mrs. Beattie says to give you a hand,' Lizzie said.

The other girl straightened and put her fists on her hips.

'Oh aye, but I don't suppose she told you where to put your box.'

She dried her hands on her rough sacking apron and hurried into the house, along the corridor and up the stairs, with Lizzie close behind. At the top they turned left, then continued to the end of the passageway.

'There's your room,' she said, as she threw the door wide. 'Come down to the kitchen when you're ready.'

Your room. The words repeated themselves in Lizzie's head. A room to herself, for the first time in her life. She glanced round, taking in the single bed, the plain wooden table holding a basin and ewer, and the narrow wardrobe. After tidying away her few possessions, Lizzie made her way back to the kitchen.

'Help yourself to a cuppie,' said the maid from her seat at the table. 'She won't be bothering us for a while.'

Lizzie poured herself some tea, sat down and asked, 'They'll be at their lessons just now, then?'

'They get their lessons from half past nine till half past eleven, and then she has them again after they've had their dinner. It works out fine – lets you get on with your work in peace.'

'You'll know I'm Lizzie, then.'

'Aye, she told me that much. I'm Agnes.'

'You'll have been here for a while?'

'Too bliddy long, if you ask me.' Agnes sniffed, pursed her lips and continued, 'I came here at the same time they did, a bit more than a year ago. The little one arrived soon after.' She gave a short laugh. 'She was queer enough before he came, but she's been a damt sight queerer since.'

Lizzie was intrigued. 'What do you mean, "queer"?'

Agnes nursed her cup between her hands and gazed ahead.

'Well, it's not just one thing – more a lot of little things. But you'll soon see for yourself that she's queer, right enough.' She set her cup on the table. 'Come on, it's time the washing was out. By the way,' she nodded towards a closed door, 'that's where she keeps the food – such as it is. It's locked and she keeps the key herself.'

Lizzie wondered why anyone would keep food locked away.

'And the door next to it?' asked Lizzie.

'Oh, that's not locked. It's just an empty cupboard. Not a damt thing in it.'

They were pegging out the last of the clothes when a low, raucous sound made Lizzie turn her head. A seagull stood on the roof of the washhouse. It seemed to be staring right at her with its strange, unblinking eyes and Lizzie shivered.

'That one's a good bit from the sea,' Agnes commented with a sniff. 'Come on, then.' And they started down the hill, leaving the washing snapping on the line.

'Time to put on the dinner, what there is of it,' Agnes grumbled. She handed a few small potatoes to Lizzie. 'The knife's in the drawer over there.'

Dinner was almost ready when the door that led from the hallway creaked open. Mrs. Beattie came in and went over to check the small pot of stew and the potatoes that were simmering on the stove. The children had followed her in and now stood silently by the door. Lizzie admired their clothes. The girl wore a velveteen dress with a lace collar, the boy a jacket and knickerbockers of fine suiting. Their mother spoke to Lizzie.

'You can take them back to the sitting-room when they have eaten.' On her way out she added, 'And they *have* washed their hands.'

The children stood mute. Lizzie went over to them.

'Come away and have your dinner. You're Thomas, and you're Christianna, aren't you?'

She took a hand in each of hers, and led them to the table, where Agnes had divided the food onto four plates.

'Is that all there is?' Lizzie asked.

'Aye, that's it – apart from a drop of pudding,' replied Agnes, giving her usual sniff of disapproval. 'It's just as well I go home at night. Your cousin Freda was close enough to Winfield to go home at night as well. If we were depending on the food we get here, we'd starve to death. What's left out for us wouldn't feed a bird.'

As Lizzie ate, she tried not to think of meals in her own home – the heaped bowls of potatoes and vegetables, the chatter and the banter.

The door creaked again, and a man's voice said, 'Oh, Mrs. Beattie's not here then.'

'No, Mr. Beattie,' said Agnes. 'I think she's upstairs with the baby.'

As the door closed, Agnes said, 'The poor man doesn't have his troubles to seek with that one.' And she jerked her head towards the ceiling.

Lizzie glanced anxiously at the children, but they were both engrossed in eating their meal.

'Is that good, now?' she asked them. Both nodded without looking up.

After they had finished the meagre amount of cornflour pudding, the children sat with their hands in their laps until Lizzie said, 'Well, time to go back to your mother.'

Again, she took each child by the hand, then walked them along the corridor. She knocked lightly on the sitting-room door and, on hearing 'Come in,' went in and led the children past the baby's cot where he lay asleep, to their mother, who sat at the window writing in a book. As Lizzie stood there, Mrs. Beattie slipped the book into the table drawer, locked the drawer and dropped the key into the deep pocket in her skirt. Then, withdrawing her hand a little, she seemed to be looking at something else that she held there. Down into the pocket went her hand again, and she withdrew it, now empty.

'It's good to see you have been properly brought up,' she said. 'I've known people who would walk straight into a room, without even a knock.'

Lizzie smiled appreciatively, but her employer had already turned her attention to the children. Considering herself dismissed, Lizzie returned to the kitchen. There she spent the afternoon with Agnes, first scrubbing the tables and the floor. Agnes explained that this was done every Monday, and although Lizzie was surprised that Monday's work included emptying the drawers and scrubbing them inside as well as out, she got on with the work.

'It's real quiet here, isn't it?' Lizzie spoke her thought aloud.

'Aye.' Agnes rested her scrubbing brush for a moment. 'I like it well enough here, but I'm not so old that I couldn't be doing with a bit more fun at times.'

'You're older than me,' said Lizzie.

'Just a couple of years. I was sixteen last birthday,' said Agnes.

There came a rap at the outside door. Agnes threw her brush into the sink and swung the door open. A young lad stood there holding a small sack. He snatched his cap from his head as Agnes put her fist on her hip and said, in a slightly mocking tone of voice, 'Well, well, if it isn't the lad himself.'

Lizzie saw the boy's face flush and felt for him.

'I just thought you could use a few potatoes off the farm,' he said.

'Well, that's right damt good of you,' said Agnes. 'Lizzie, come and meet Geordie.'

Lizzie smiled at the lad and said shyly, 'Hello, Geordie.'

'Hello, Lizzie,' he said. 'I see you're busy.'

Agnes lifted an eyebrow. 'And what else is there to do around here but be busy?'

'We could take a walk tonight,' he offered.

'A walk? A walk to where?'

'Have you ever been up the hill, past the manse?'

'Aye, just about every day, with the washing.'

'No, I mean to the very top. It's real bonny. You can see right across to the sea.'

'Well, I can't stay here all day chatting. I've work to do. If I'm finished at the usual time, I'll see you at the bottom of the hill path.'

Lizzie saw the boy's face light up just before Agnes slammed the door shut.

– 3 –

Bedtime

Later that day, Mrs. Beattie appeared in the kitchen as the two girls and the children were finishing their sparse evening meal. She came over to the table and stood there with hands clasped.

'Now then, Lizzie, you can take the children to the book room and do some reading with them, and be sure they behave themselves.' The door creaked as she left.

After Agnes had left for home, Lizzie walked the children along the passage to what Mrs. Beattie had called 'the book room'. Inside there was a table, some hard chairs and a bookcase with a variety of reading material.

'Will we have *Sunshine Hours*?' asked Lizzie. The children merely looked at each other. By now, Lizzie was beginning to wonder if they were 'right in their heads', as her mother would have put it. But she took down the book, sat at the little table with the children and read the first poem to them. It was hard to tell from their expressions whether or not they were enjoying it – or if they even understood what she was saying. Lizzie handed the book to the boy.

'You try the next one, Thomas.'

There was little emotion in his voice as he read, but he read surprisingly well. Then Lizzie tried Christianna with a very simple poem and, young as she was, she managed to read it. They were part way through the book when Mrs. Beattie came in. Lizzie noticed that she was clenching and unclenching her hand within the pocket of her dark dress.

'And have they behaved themselves?' she asked.

'Oh aye, Mrs. Beattie. They've been very good – and they're real quick at the reading.'

'Well, about their bedtime,' Mrs. Beattie continued, ignoring Lizzie's praise, 'I was wondering if I'll just put them to bed myself as usual.'

She looked towards the window, then back to Lizzie.

'On the other hand, you might as well start as you're going to continue. Their bedtime is eight-thirty, *no* later. Just see that they wash their hands and faces in their room before you bed them.'

She went out without a glance at the children.

'Well, bairns,' said Lizzie, 'it's nearly that time now, so we'll just go upstairs and you can show me where your room is.'

She felt relief as they climbed the stairs and walked along the corridor. The two unresponsive children were more wearying to her than all the naughtiness and energy of her own younger sisters. Thomas and Christianna duly washed their hands and faces in the basin of water that Lizzie had poured from the ewer, then undressed modestly with their backs to each other. Lizzie was appalled to see their thin little bodies as they donned their nightgowns. She turned away to place the basin near the door, lest they should see the look on her face.

My God, she thought, *if those were two of my da's calfies, he'd have had them put down out of their misery.*

'Will we say our prayers now?' asked Thomas, once they were in their beds.

'Oh... oh aye,' she answered.

She barely heard the words of their prayers. All she could think of was the sight of their ribs and their stick-like arms and legs.

'Goodnight, then,' she said. 'I'll see you in the morning.'

Tired though she was, Lizzie lay awake in her bed going over the events of the day. Mrs. Beattie's abrupt manner was something she would have to get used to. She thought of the children too – so bright and yet so lacking in spirit.

She had fallen into a light sleep when a soft tapping awoke her. Her eyes opened a little, then closed again. The sound came again, a little louder. This time she was wide awake. When the tapping next came, it seemed to come from the window, and superstitious fear gripped her for a moment. But she slipped her feet out of bed, crossed the cold floor and saw the tree outside. There was just enough breeze to produce the intermittent tapping of its branches against the window-pane. Lizzie went back to bed, pulled the blankets up to her neck and was soon asleep.

Visitors

Lizzie became accustomed to the routine of the manse and the unrelenting cleaning of things already clean. The children stayed as thin as ever, despite the little extra food that Agnes, and sometimes Lizzie, managed to give them. Lizzie herself was almost constantly hungry, and she still missed home and the warmth of her family. She was gratified, though, to notice an occasional smile flicker over Christianna's face when Mrs. Beattie handed the children over to her.

Visitors were few. Those who came to see the minister or his wife were seldom seen by Lizzie. At the sound of the doorbell, Agnes would hurry to the front door and usher them into the 'best' room. Later, Lizzie would learn who the visitors were and Agnes's opinions of each and every one – opinions that were often accompanied by a sniff. Lizzie was sometimes torn between shock and laughter at some of Agnes's descriptions. One time, she pulled Lizzie from the kitchen to the front door to peep round the corner of the house and watch the departing visitors.

'That's Big Annie with her two bairns, looking for something for nothing. Mind you, she's got her troubles with a man like she has. Tommy's one of them that would like to get up, but his backside won't let him.' Seeing Lizzie's look of bemusement, she explained.

'Och, he's full of airs and graces, but there's no work in him. He'll aye take the easiest road. But that's two fine bairns she has there. The little boy's like his mam, roly-poly and easy-going, though a bit spoiled I'd say. But the older one now, she's a grand wee lass.'

Another day, Lizzie heard about the Thomsons. 'A couple of long drips, that two. They suck up to Mrs. Beattie something terrible. There's never a month passes but they're here pleading poverty. They've got a bit of land, but they're just too mean to get enough help to farm it right. And they wear nothing but black. You'd think they were aye dressed for a funeral.'

And then there was Babbie-Ann. The two girls were at the usual Monday scrubbing-out of the kitchen when Lizzie heard about Babbie-Ann. 'That was her at the door just now. I took her through to the room and skedaddled. You try to keep out of the way of that one. She's got eyes like a hawk – sees everything and speaks ill of the best of folk.' Agnes picked up a clean drawer. 'And when she can't find any gossip, she'll make it up. She's a coarse-tongued old bitch.' Here she pursed her lips, sniffed and banged the drawer back into place.

One morning when Lizzie was alone in the kitchen drying the last of the dishes, there was a knock on the back door. She opened it, but with the sun in her eyes, all she could see was a tall deformed-looking figure. She was about to slam the door shut when the figure pushed past her into the kitchen and revealed itself as a gypsy woman with a pack on her shoulder.

'Is Agnes about?' she asked.

The inner door squeaked open, and Agnes came in.

'Well, Jean, it's yourself. It's a while since we've seen you.'

'Aye,' responded the woman. 'We stayed longer inland this year. One of the bairns wasn't well and we couldn't travel till he was better. So you'll maybe be needing a few things by now?' She swung the pack-blanket from her shoulder and spread it out on the floor. Lizzie caught a glimpse of coloured ribbons and cotton reels. As the woman knelt to set out her goods, the back door opened a little.

Agnes went over and opened the door wider, and Mrs. Buchan stepped in. She dropped her creel by the door and, hands to her back, straightened up. Dolly followed her inside. Agnes turned to Lizzie. 'My, I was nearly forgetting. Mrs. Beattie wants you. The little bairn has woken up and she's wanting you to take him and let her get on with the other two.'

Lizzie returned with the child in her arms. 'He's not so easy for Mrs. Beattie to look after now that he's started walking.'

Dolly beamed at the baby and moved forward with arms outstretched, saying, 'Dolly, dolly.'

'Come away now, Dolly,' came her mother's voice. 'Mad keen on babies, she is,' she said in an aside to Lizzie then, to her daughter, 'That's not your doll. Here's *your* doll,' and she picked up the bundle of wrapped cloths that Dolly had dropped.

The smile left Dolly's face. As she turned from the baby,

the woman Jean stood up before her, blocking her way. She looked at Dolly with a strange intensity. 'Eh, lassie, lassie.' Her head went slowly from side to side. 'There's death in your face.'

Dolly, uncomprehending, stared back, until she felt her mother's hand pulling her to safety behind her.

'What do you think you're doing, scaring my Dolly like that? Get away out of here with your devil's eyes!'

'Aye, I'll get away,' said the dark-haired woman as she gathered up her wares and swung the bundle once more over her shoulder. 'But I can only say what I see, and I see death in that lassie's face.'

Dolly's mother made a dash for her, but the woman was out and away before she could reach her.

'Come away, Mrs. Buchan, come away.' Agnes put an arm round the woman's shoulder and guided her to the table. 'Sit down and have a cup of tea while I have a look at your fish. I've put by a few eggs for you. And pay no attention to that woman. It's all havers.'

She pushed a plate of oatcakes across the table. 'Here, have a bite to eat with your tea.'

'No, thank you, Agnes. We'll not have anything to eat. Dolly's getting heavy enough these days.'

And so the woman was soothed, and fish and eggs were exchanged, before she left with her daughter.

– 5 –

Babbie-Ann

Higher up the hill, a solitary man watched as a figure appeared from the back of the manse. The figure walked, then ran lightly to where the sheets lay spread on the grass in the sunshine. The man turned away and walked on up the hill.

Lizzie stood beside the sheets, now dry and dazzling white on the grass. As she waited for Agnes to join her, she became aware of a voice that seemed to come from a dip further up the hill, and she moved towards it. Looking down into the dip, she saw a small hut. Outside the hut, a man bent his head towards something he held in his hand. As Lizzie squinted into the sunshine, she saw the head of a small bird.

'You're all right now, my wee birdie. All better.' The voice was soft, but when he looked up and saw Lizzie, it changed. 'Away you go now, and don't come back here annoying me anymore.' And he raised and opened his hand. The bird flew up and away. Scowling, the man limped hurriedly out of the dip and on up the hillside, rousing the noisy crows from the high trees, before he disappeared from view.

Agnes came from the house, and Lizzie waited until they had each lifted the corners of the first sheet and started to fold it before she asked, 'Did you see that man?'

'Who, Daniel? Och, he's aye tinkerin' about at something or other.'

'He didn't seem too pleased to see me.'

They continued folding as Agnes said, 'I've heard he was nice enough at one time. A real cheery soul. Got married to a lassie from inland – round about Huntly way, I believe. Anyway, he thought the world of her.'

They finished folding the sheet. Agnes laid it into the basket, and they picked up the corners of the next sheet as she continued.

'As things turned out, their bairn started to come too early. The doctor lived close by and Daniel, he ran hell-for-leather for the doctor, fell and broke his leg in the dark, but kept on running. It never healed right, after that. As for the poor lassie, she died giving birth, and the bairn soon after. That's when Daniel changed. Stopped speaking to folk. He's never been heard to laugh since – just turned in on himself, as you might say. Stays on his own in a house above the crows' wood there.'

She nodded her head in the direction that Daniel had taken. Lizzie pondered on the story as they each took a handle of the heavy basket and carried it down the hill.

At the kitchen door, Agnes elbowed open the latch and kicked a washing basket out of her way. After putting the sheets away upstairs, the girls returned to the kitchen. Agnes picked up the washing basket that she'd kicked and thumped it down on the table.

'This is one of Doris's "odds and ends" baskets, as she calls them.'

Lizzie, though horrified at the use of their employer's first name, made no reply.

'Look at this – all shrunken.' Agnes had picked up a man's sock by the toe. 'What the hell we're supposed to do with that rubbish, I do not know. Most of it's just fit for the fire.' She picked up a garment and displayed the holes in it. 'But wait a minute... wait a minute. I've just had a thought. There's one or two woollen things here. Shrunken or not, I wonder...'

Her musings were cut short by the sound of the doorbell, and she dropped the articles back into the basket and went off. Lizzie occupied herself by preparing the usual small meal until Agnes returned, pulling Dolly with her. She took the girl to the back door.

'Away home now, Dolly. Your mam'll be looking for you.'

She waited to see that the girl was headed in the right direction before closing the door.

'That was Babbie-Ann at the front door. When I took her into the best room, there was Dolly with her arms wrapped round the minister, looking up at him as if he was God Almighty. When Babbie-Ann saw them, she went straight out of the house without a word and a face like thunder. God knows what she's going to make of it, but I tell you she'll make *something* of it, that's certain.'

Mrs. Beattie, unaware of the little drama that had taken place, told the children to go to the kitchen for their midday meal, and closed the sitting-room door behind them as they left. Plunging her hand into the pocket of her dress, she withdrew a small object and carried it to the window. As she stood with the object in her palm, moving her hand a little this way and that, admiring its dull gleam in the sunlight, her thoughts went back to her own childhood. She remembered sitting on the plush settee, feeling very proud in her new dress. The nanny had taken special care of her blonde hair and ringlets that day. She had looked at herself in the mirror, admiring the rounded face and prettily plump figure, so unlike her younger brother Andrew, who was thin and dark-haired. Then she had sat with him, fidgeting a little, impatient for her mother to come and show her approval. At last the door had opened and her beloved mother stepped in. Doris lowered her eyes in delicious anticipation.

'Well, don't you look nice, darling! All ready to go to Grandma's?'

Doris looked up in surprise. She had heard nothing of a visit to Grandma's. But her mother was looking at Andrew. She had taken his hand and walked with him to the door. 'Bye-bye, Doris. Be good for Nanny,' she had called as mother and son left the room.

Doris had walked to the window and watched as her mother helped the boy onto the trap and nodded her bonneted head towards the driver. He gave a shake of the reins, and they moved off.

It seemed to Doris that she had always been troubled by such memories. Since the birth of her youngest child, there were whole days when the memories crowded in on her, reminding her over and over again of her own worthlessness. Doris lifted her head. Things were going to be different for *her* children. She would make sure that they would never be like she was as a child – fat and stupid – and she slipped the coloured object back into the pocket of her skirt.

– 6 –

A Present for Dolly

John Beattie, too, was thinking of the past. He frowned, trying hard to ignore the feelings of guilt that rose within him. Pushing his paperwork to one side he sat, elbow on desk and chin in hand, as his thoughts returned to when he first met the girl who became his wife.

John had first seen Doris from the pulpit in Edinburgh when he was standing in for the local minister. She sat with her mother and brother, eyes downcast, as she listened to his sermon. Later, as he shook hands with the congregation at the church door, he had been attracted by her plump prettiness and clear blue eyes. He remembered noticing the tendril of blonde hair that had escaped from her bonnet and lay nestled against her cheek.

Soon after that first meeting he had made a pastoral call on the family. A maidservant had led him to the elegant sitting-room, where he was welcomed by Mrs. Groat. She indicated a chair for him, quite close to where Doris sat, then returned to the settee to sit beside her son.

'How like his father he is. He never knew his father, you know.' She looked with sorrow at the boy. 'We lost his father when Andrew was just months old. My poor boy was frail from birth.'

She gave a sigh and looked back at them. 'When he was born, the doctor said that we'd be lucky if he survived at all, so you can see how it has been for me. Never a day goes by that I don't fear for him.' She shook her head slowly in emphasis and patted the lad's knee.

'Shall I get Maisie to bring some tea, Mother?' Doris asked.

'Yes, dear. That'll be nice,' Mrs. Groat answered absently.

'And has his condition never improved?' asked John, for the child, though hardly robust, looked healthy enough.

'He's a *little* better these days. In fact, the doctor has said that there's really nothing to worry about now but, to this day,' she leaned toward John, 'I worry if he looks the least bit pale. I'm afraid the habit has become ingrained,' and she smiled a sad little smile.

John cleared his throat. 'And Doris?' he asked.

'Oh, Doris is fine. She's very healthy, and clever at her lessons too, but poor Andrew,' and again she looked with sympathy at her son, 'well, of course we can't expect too much of him.'

That visit had been the first of many, and by the time his temporary post had come to an end, John was deeply in love. With Mrs. Groat's blessing, Doris and John were married. John was given his first living in the same city, and Thomas and Christianna were born there. They were all, at first, very happy. But this had changed gradually. John noticed that the children were not thriving, and Doris herself had lost that pleasant roundness. Also, on her frequent visits to her mother, Doris would come back silent and looking pinched. It seemed to John that it might be best to get Doris away from a situation that was causing her some kind of grief, and perhaps the children would thrive away from the city air.

And so they had come here to the manse, and it was here that he had discovered the real reason for the children's near-emaciation. It was not the lack of fresh air, but Doris's insistence that they mustn't eat too much. He had sensed that this obsession, for he could call it no less, stemmed from her own childhood in some way.

But, despite John's best efforts, Doris's confidence was fragile. On the few occasions that he had attempted to broach the subject, Doris had looked so distressed – and on one occasion, almost wild – that he had abandoned any hope of change.

His reverie was interrupted by a tap on the door. He sat back in his chair and to his call of 'Come in,' Lizzie came in with his afternoon tea on a tray. She set it on his desk, and he gave an appreciative 'Ah.' Lizzie paused on her way out as he said, 'Lizzie, you and Agnes work hard. I must see Mrs. Beattie about letting you both have some time off.'

It was the following week that Lizzie and Agnes, in their promised time off, took the road to Mrs. Buchan's house. Lizzie had made a doll from some washed-out cotton, sewing on two eyes and a smiling mouth, while Agnes had knitted a multi-coloured shawl for it from the 'odds and ends' basket. The sun was warm, though a breeze blew their long skirts about them.

'That doesn't look too promising,' said Agnes, nodding towards the clouds that were building up on the horizon.

'Aye, there'll be rain before night, I'm thinking,' Lizzie agreed.

Mrs. Buchan welcomed them with pleasure. 'Come away in and sit down. You'll have a cup of tea?'

The girls smiled over at Dolly as she sat in her rocking chair by the fire, then settled themselves as Dolly's mother poured water into a teapot from the kettle that hung from the hook over the open fire. After handing them their cups of tea, she sat down by the fireside across from Dolly. They talked of the weather as the woman waited politely for them to come round to the reason for their visit. After a proper interval, Agnes got up and placed her parcel on the older woman's knees, saying, 'This is for Dolly, Mrs. Buchan.' Lizzie put her own parcel on the arm of the woman's chair, adding, 'And this one as well,' and the girls sat down again.

'What's this, then?' asked Mrs. Buchan. She opened the first parcel, then the second. 'Oh my! Dolly, come and see what the ladies have brought you.' Dolly ambled over. 'Here you are, Dolly. It's for you.'

Dolly's rounded arms reached out and, after one or two fumbling attempts, had the doll wrapped in its shawl. She carried it to the corner of the room to a little cradle and, after taking out the bundle of rags that lay there and dropping them on the floor, she laid the new doll gently inside. After a moment, Dolly picked it up again and went back to her chair, where she sat with the doll in her arms, humming tunelessly and rocking. Now and then she would stop, look down at her new 'dolly', smile, then set off rocking and humming again, greatly content.

'That's real good of you both,' said her mother.

'You'd think she was cuddling a real bairn,' said Lizzie.

'Oh, God forbid.' Mrs. Buchan frowned. 'I've done my best for Dolly all these years, but I just couldn't face another lifetime of it.'

A little while later the two girls said their goodbyes. As they left the cottage it started to rain and, by the time they parted, Agnes to go to her home and Lizzie to return to the manse, the rain was heavy.

The cloud-darkened sky made it difficult for Lizzie to see the way ahead. After stumbling along for some long time, she was relieved to see, through the now teeming rain, a flicker of light coming from the direction of the manse. Her hands finally found the opening in the low wall, and she turned into the path. What looked like a lantern was bobbing on the hill that led to the house. A little higher there was a second lantern. She could hear voices calling, and recognised one as the minister's.

'Is that you, Lizzie?' His voice was raised against the noise of the rain. 'Will you go in and stay with Mrs. Beattie?'

Nearer the house, as she passed the other lantern-bearer, she shouted, 'What's wrong, Daniel?'

'Ach, the woman's been out in this downpour looking for some damn fool brooch, and the little bairn got out and is lost,' he roared back at her.

Lizzie ran the last few steps through mud and puddles and entered the house.

– 7 –

The Search

In the bedroom, Mrs. Beattie stood by the empty cot.

'Oh, Mrs. Beattie, you're all wet,' said Lizzie, ignoring her own sodden state. The woman showed no sign that Lizzie had spoken to her. She seemed to be looking into some distant place.

'Come and have a cup of tea,' said Lizzie. Putting her hand on her employer's arm, she led her downstairs and into the kitchen, where she eased her onto a chair and lit a lamp.

The back door was open. As Lizzie went to close it, she heard the hens squawking loudly, and knew that the henhouse door must be open. She stepped out, slipping on the wet cobbles, and was about to close the door on the hens when she thought she heard a thin wail amongst the din. Stooping into the henhouse, she could just make out the shape of the child's white nightdress on the floor. As she reached down, the claws of a frightened hen tore across the back of her hand. She shook it off and groped forward until her hands touched the baby's face. It was covered with something wet and sticky. Fighting down a wave of nausea, she picked up the crying child, bobbed her head down at the low doorway and hurried to the kitchen.

Mrs. Beattie still sat as if she could neither hear nor see.

Lizzie brought the child close to the lamp on the table. When she saw his face, she gave a half sob of relief. The child's face was streaked with raw egg. Through his fingers dripped the same mess and, as he opened his hand, Lizzie saw the remains of the shell. After wiping the mess from his hands and face, she carried him along the corridor and opened the front door, where she stood on the top step gasping and said, 'Mr. Beattie, I've got him.' Then, realising that her voice was too low to be heard through the still-heavy rain, she took a deep breath and called, 'Mr. Beattie! I've got the bairn! He's all right!'

That evening, John Beattie sat at the table in the drawing-room, his head bowed. The doctor stood near him.

'Well, I can find nothing physically wrong with your wife, but what on earth possessed her, man, to be outside on a night like this?'

'It was the brooch she was looking for.'

'Brooch! Brooch!' The look of incredulity on the doctor's face asked for some kind of explanation.

'It was a brooch her mother had given to her. She set great store by it.' He wiped his hand across his brow and looked up at the doctor. 'You see, she always felt that she'd never lived up to her mother's expectations. That brooch meant more to her than just an ornament. She kept it with her all the time.'

'Aye,' said the doctor, 'and by dwelling on the past, she's damned near lost the present, to say nothing of the bairn's life. As things stand, she's fairly lost her reason – for the time being at any rate.'

John shook his head slowly. 'I blame myself. If only I could have done more for her.'

The doctor put a hand on the man's shoulder. 'Now, John, there's nobody on earth could have done more for her than yourself.'

He moved away then turned to look at John again. 'You mentioned her mother. They're on speaking terms, I take it?'

'Oh aye.' John sighed.

'Would she come here if you asked her?'

'I've no doubt she would.'

'Then that's my advice to you. Send for her mother.'

– 8 –

Changes at the Big House

On the following morning, as Agnes walked towards the kitchen door to begin her day's work, she noticed that the hens were already out. They jerked slowly around the little courtyard, making the soft 'churring' sound that they usually made after being fed.

Lizzie must have been up early, she thought.

She was surprised to find Lizzie at the table feeding the baby as the children ate their porridge. 'What...?' she began, but Lizzie frowned and shook her head.

'That's right, bairns. Just finish up your breakfast, and we'll see what's next.' To Agnes she said, 'Mrs. Beattie's not very well this morning. Now that you're here, I'll away and see Mr. Beattie.' She passed the baby to Agnes.

On her return, she told the children, 'Your father says that seeing as it's such a bonny morning, we should all go out.' She gave Agnes a key. 'And he's given us the key to the food cupboard, so we can have a bit of a picnic.'

Once Agnes had filled a basket, she took her knitting from the table and placed it on top of the tea-towel that covered the picnic things. Meanwhile, Lizzie had been getting the children dressed for outdoors. Now she put a shawl around her shoulders and wrapped the baby securely within her arms. They went out by the front door, crossed the road and started up the hill ahead.

'You two go on ahead then,' Lizzie said to the children, 'and keep out of the puddles.' To Agnes she said, 'What a lovely shawl this is. It probably came with them from Edinburgh.'

Once the children had run ahead, she told Agnes of the events of the previous evening. 'And do you know, Mrs. Beattie hasn't opened her mouth since. Mr. Beattie has sent for her mother.'

'I told you she wasn't right in the head,' Agnes sniffed, 'starving herself and the bairns like that, and always at the lessons, nothing but lessons.'

'Aye, there's something far wrong, right enough,' said Lizzie. 'Come on, we'll catch up with the bairns.'

As they reached the top of a rise, the sea came into view, blue and wide. Lizzie called the children, and they had their picnic in a sheltered hollow, sitting on the stones that rose from the damp grass. After they'd eaten, the children sat quietly.

'Go and play chases for a while,' Lizzie urged them. They looked at her blankly. 'Well, first Thomas has to chase Christianna till he catches her, then you, Christianna, have to chase him till you catch him. Let your sister run on a bit before you start chasing her, Thomas. She's littler than you.'

Soon the girls heard sounds of laughter as the children found each other, then started off on their chase again. Lizzie sat with the baby on her knee, while Agnes took out her knitting. 'You know,' mused Agnes, 'there's not much wrong with those bairns. They're just in need of a bit more slack, a bit of freedom, you might say – *and* a bit more feeding. They fairly made short work of their porridge this morning.'

Lizzie smiled and asked, 'What's that you're knitting?'

'My sister Jenny's having another bairn, though God knows she's got plenty already. Anyway, I'm knitting a jacket for it.'

'And what about your other sisters? We don't seem to have had time to talk about our families till now.'

'Well, Jenny's the oldest, then there's Carrie, me, and the two younger ones, Billy and Patty. And what about yourself?'

'Jane's twenty then, after me, there's Margaret and Mary and James.' They chatted on until Lizzie wrapped herself and the baby in the shawl again and stood up. 'I'd better be calling the bairns,' she said. 'It must be getting near to dinner time.'

She walked over rises and down hollows towards the sound of their voices and called them. At the top of one rise, far below, she saw a rough circle of boulders. The deep shadows amongst the tall stones contrasted with the sunlit scene, and Lizzie shivered. When Thomas and Christianna reached her, she hurried them back to where Agnes waited, basket on arm.

The next few days passed pleasantly. There were other outdoor trips, and more food on plates. Although the shadow of their mistress's illness was with them, the two girls were cheered as they saw the change in the children. They were cheered, too, that cleaning was done as necessary, and that the needless drudgery had ended.

One evening, while they were eating, the doorbell rang.

'Wonder if that's her,' said Agnes, and the door creaked as she went to find out.

'It was her, right enough,' she told Lizzie when she came back. 'She's up with Doris now. Mr. Beattie's sent for the doctor again.'

'What's she like?' Lizzie asked. 'Does Mrs. Beattie look like her?'

'Aye, you can see the resemblance, though the mother's real fancy-like. Posh hat on her head – must have cost a pretty penny.' Agnes gave a sniff.

Later, as Lizzie passed the sitting-room with the children, the door opened and Mrs. Beattie's mother stepped out, followed by the doctor.

'I'll just let myself out, Lizzie,' he said as he passed her.

Lizzie took in the rich sheen of the woman's burgundy dress, and caught the fragrance of lavender. She noticed that tears glistened in her eyes as she bent towards the children.

'You remember me, don't you – your grandma?' she asked softly. Thomas nodded. 'We're going to have plenty of time to get to know each other better.' Then, to Lizzie she added, 'I suppose it's their bedtime?'

Something in the woman's manner prompted Lizzie to answer, uncharacteristically, 'Yes, Madam.'

'Goodnight then, children. I'll see you again tomorrow.'

Lizzie felt the woman's eyes follow them as they climbed upwards, until they all three disappeared round the turn of the stairs.

– 9 –

Leaving

On Sunday, as the bells pealed calling the people to prayer, Lizzie, in her fine grey dress, walked the short distance to the church with Mr. Beattie and the children.

This was the first time that Lizzie had heard her employer speak from the pulpit and his words held her. There was a whispering from somewhere behind. Turning her head a little, she saw Babbie-Ann between two other women, all in their best Sunday black. Babbie-Ann would look beneath her brows towards the pulpit, then return to her whispering. The black feather in her hat bobbed in time with her emphatic words. Someone gave a short 'Sh!' and the whispering stopped.

Service over, Mr. Beattie stood outside shaking hands with his parishioners. Lizzie felt a bit out of place as she took Mrs. Beattie's usual place, standing behind him with the children. Babbie-Ann and her two cronies passed without shaking his hand or even looking at him. Lizzie watched them until they stopped at the church gate, where the whispering started again, accompanied by covert glances towards the minister. The last of the people had drifted away and Mr. Beattie was ready to leave, and still the three women stood at the gate.

He passed them with a nod, but as Lizzie reached them she heard Babbie-Ann mutter, 'Imagine him standing there preaching after taking advantage of that poor, simple lassie. Little wonder that his wife's gone off her head.'

After telling the children to go ahead with their father, Lizzie turned to the women.

'You don't know what you're talking about, for I stay in the house, and I know what a good man he is.'

The women looked at each other with tightened lips. This time Lizzie raised her voice. 'And as for you, Babbie-Ann, you're nothing but a coarse-tongued bitch!'

The young girl was almost at the manse before she felt calmer, but the calm was followed by a feeling of dismay at what she'd said.

Agnes stepped into the kitchen the following morning, hung her coat on the peg behind the door, then looked at Lizzie.

'Well, and what's the matter with *you* today?'

'Oh Agnes, I've let my tongue run away with me. I don't know what got into me.'

'Well, sit down, sit down. It won't sound any better standing up, whatever it is.'

Lizzie slipped into a chair at the table and Agnes sat down across from her.

'I don't know where to start.'

'This'll be something that happened yesterday?' Agnes prompted.

'Aye. It started in the kirk.' Agnes listened until Lizzie

finished with 'And in the end, oh Agnes – I told her she was a coarse-tongued old bitch.'

'Did you now? You called her that, did you? Well, if you remember, that's the very same words I called her to you, when you first came. Lizzie, lass, I think you'll have to watch the kind of company you keep,' Agnes said solemnly.

Then, looking at Lizzie from the corner of her eye, she smiled. The smile grew wider, and she began to laugh. Still laughing, she bent forward then threw herself backwards and, with a shriek, went into another bout of laughter. Lizzie began to laugh too. Eventually they paused for breath, wiping the tears from their eyes.

'Oh, if you'd just seen her face, Agnes. Dumbfounded wasn't the word for it.'

'I can just picture it. Was it like this?' Agnes opened her eyes wide, and let her mouth drop open.

'Aye,' shrieked a delighted Lizzie. 'That was her, right enough.' And they fell to laughing again.

At last, Lizzie put her hands on the table and stood up. 'Come on, Agnes. It'll be nearly dinner time before we know where we are.' And she turned towards the heap of vegetables on the sink with a lighter heart.

Mr. Beattie's head appeared round the kitchen door.

'I wonder, Lizzie, if you'll come and see me in the study after you've had your meal. And maybe you'll come too, Agnes. Mrs. Beattie's mother will take the children.'

In the study, the two girls sat side by side facing Mr. Beattie, who leaned a little forward, hands clasped on the desk.

'Well, no doubt you'll be wondering why you're here. You know that Mrs. Beattie is far from well just now.' He looked down at his hands for a moment. 'The doctor has said that she'll recover more quickly in her home town with her mother to care for her. That means, of course, that we'll all be returning to Edinburgh as soon as possible. I've been fortunate in finding a replacement for myself at such short notice. The new minister is a single man. Now, would either of you be willing to stay on at the manse?' The girls glanced at each other. Agnes was first to speak.

'It would suit me to stay on, Mr. Beattie. With just the new minister here, I could manage fine, and still have time to help my mother after my sister gets married.'

'And you, Lizzie?'

'Oh, I'm sure to find work. There's a few families nearby that could do with a hand.'

'That's put my mind at rest, then.' He stood up, crossed the room and held the door open for them.

Lizzie and Agnes spent the rest of that week packing the family's possessions. The minister had matters to attend to, but Daniel proved helpful, though as surly as ever. Except for the day that Dolly turned up. As the girls and Daniel packed Old Tom's cart with the last of the boxes, Dolly came walking slowly up the road towards them. Lizzie saw that she was heavier than ever, her pinny drawn tight across her stomach.

Dolly moved towards Daniel. His voice was gentle as he said, 'Na, na, Dolly. We're busy just now. Away you go home now, there's a good lass.'

As Dolly, still smiling, turned away to walk back, Lizzie noticed a family of gypsies drawing near. They passed on the other side of the road, and she wondered if they would be visiting her mother at the farm. She suddenly realised how much she was looking forward to going home. Agnes surveyed the packed cart, fists on hips. 'Well, that looks real tidy. The train folk'll get at that lot easy enough. Are you ready to go yourself?'

'Aye. My box is in the front with Tom.' Old Tom was to drop Lizzie off at the farm on his way to the station.

Surprisingly, Daniel came forward to help her up to her seat. Lizzie, averting her eyes from his now scowling face as he handed her up, noticed a red birthmark on the lighter skin of his forearm. *It's just like the leaf of a birch tree*, she thought. Without waiting to wave them off, Daniel limped away and made for the path that led to his home.

John Beattie, coming down the manse path, called to them to wait. He thanked Lizzie for her help and handed her an envelope.

'There's a reference in there for you, Lizzie, and something from the children's grandmother.'

Old Tom touched his cap to the minister, slapped the reins lightly on the big horse's back, and they moved off, with Lizzie waving back to Agnes and Mr. Beattie.

As soon as the cart had swayed round the first bend in the

road, Lizzie bent down, unlaced her boots and eased them off. Wriggling her toes on the cool boards, she sat back and looked ahead, towards home.

– 10 –

Dolly

As Lizzie pushed open the door that led into the farmhouse kitchen, she could smell the delicious aroma of her mother's cooking. Her father was already eating, while the three children sat waiting eagerly for their mother to fill their plates.

'Lizzie, you're home!' said her mother. 'Come away in.'

The two young girls greeted her noisily, and her little brother joined in. Their father quietened them with a few words.

'Sit in when you're ready,' continued her mother. 'We're having stovies tonight.'

Lizzie left her box by the door, washed her hands at the sink and joined her family.

'You look like you need that,' said her mother, placing a dish of steaming food in front of Lizzie. 'My, but you're thin.'

Lizzie smiled and started to eat the succulent mix of roast beef scraps cooked with onions and potatoes in gravy. Later, she would tell her mother of her experiences at the Big House.

She soon settled back into her old life at the farm. One evening, as she was throwing feed to the hens, she heard a soft tread.

'I heard you were back, Lizzie.'

She recognised the voice before she turned round. It was Donald – the same bonny blue eyes and fair hair; but there was something else there, something she had never seen before – a kind of weakness beneath his easy manner. Looking down at the now empty dish in her hand, she said carefully, 'Donald, I don't think I'll be going out with you anymore.' She looked up at him. 'You see, I'd just be keeping company with you out of habit. My heart wouldn't be in it.'

'Ah well, Lizzie. If that's how you feel.'

'Aye, that's how I feel.'

He looked away, then back at her. 'Well, cheerio then, Lizzie.'

'Cheerio, Donald.'

She watched him walk away, hands in pockets.

'Lizzie, are you there?' It was her father's voice, calling from the open door of the byre.

'Aye, Da.'

'Come and give me a hand here, will you?'

She followed him into the dim, straw-smelling byre. He took a lantern from its hook on the wall.

'Will you hold the light, lass? Rosie here's having a hard time of it, pushing out her calf.'

She held the lantern high as her father swept the cow's tail aside and grasped the two protruding legs beneath. The cow's head swung round, and Lizzie saw its eyes, bulged with the effort of straining. It bellowed in pain as the next contraction came, but the farmer's sure hands and strong arms pulled steadily with the contraction and the calf slithered out. The lantern trembled in Lizzie's hand. She had long known about the process of birthing but had never been quite this close to it.

Once the calf was on its feet and suckling, her father reached for the lantern.

'That calf was a bit big for her,' he said. 'She's been trying for a while. But she'll be fine now.'

The huge afterbirth dropped from the cow and lay in a bloody heap. A strange, sweetish smell filled Lizzie's nostrils. Her father's voice seemed to come from a distance. 'Are you all right, Lizzie? I think you'd better go back to the house.'

Lizzie stumbled outside and stood leaning back against the byre wall. Eyes closed, she took deep breaths of the fresh, cool air. The sun was setting, and when she opened her eyes again, the sky to the west was streaked blood-red and crimson, staining the scene around her. A puff of wind blew a ball of dry grass over her bare feet, and then she was running towards the lighted windows of the farmhouse, calling, 'Mam! Mam!'

At Winfield, earlier that day, Mrs. Buchan had been ready to set off with Dolly, when Dolly had stopped just inside the door of the cottage.

'Oh, come on now, Dolly. You know I don't like leaving you at home on your own.'

Her mother took her hand, but Dolly pulled away and shook her head.

'Well, I'll just have to go on by myself. Will you go to bed, then, if you're not feeling well?'

Dolly nodded, and Mrs. Buchan swung the creel onto her back and left.

But Dolly was restless. She would sit in her rocking chair, get up and walk around aimlessly, then return to the chair. After one of these wanderings, she stopped by the bed and started to undress. She had only taken off her underpants when the restlessness seized her again. Picking up her doll, still wrapped in its knitted shawl, she stepped out into the sunshine, leaving the door swinging open behind her.

Dolly trudged along the road, her feet carrying her towards the minister's house and on up the hill. As she reached the cool of the trees there came a pain in her back, then a sudden gush of water between her legs. Dolly hadn't wet herself for many years, for which she was proud, and here she was wetting herself.

Whimpering, she walked through last year's dead leaves, then stumbled and fell between the roots of a tree. The pain now overwhelmed her, and she moaned. There was something between her legs. Struggling to sit, she pulled up the skirt of her dress, and reached for the baby that lay on the ground. Her doll rolled away as she picked up the shawl and wrapped it round the infant. Dolly gazed at it, cradled in her arm in the flickering sunlight, unaware that her life's blood was trickling from her. She smiled and said softly, 'Dolly… dolly…' before she lay back and closed her eyes for the last time.

– 11 –

Gypsies

High in the blue sky, the shrill chirruping of a lark grew fainter as the bird rose, then stopped abruptly as it dropped to the lush meadow below. Agnes sat on a drystone wall, her back to the skylark's meadow, her feet dangling above the wild primroses that sunned themselves at the bottom of the wall.

'Well, you'd better get to the point now that you've got me here. I haven't got all day.'

Geordie shifted from one foot to the other. 'Well, Agnes...'

'Aye?' She frowned.

'Well, Agnes, we've been going out for a while now.' He paused, then hurried on, 'I was wondering if it wasn't time we thought about getting married.'

A movement on the road below caught her eye. Big Annie was walking hand-in-hand with her small son. Kirsten walked in front. Annie gave the girl's shoulder a push at every few steps, keeping her ahead.

'Well, Agnes?'

Agnes swivelled to look at him with a frown. 'Married? Did you say married?'

'I've got an offer of a tied house at Drydykes on the under-standing I'll be a married man before long.'

'Well, God knows there's little enough to do in the Big House with just the new minister there, and him a single man.' The smile left Geordie's face when she added, 'But on the other hand, my sister gets married this year, and maybe my mother'll be needing a bit of help once Carrie's away.'

'But the house, Agnes. Mr. Nicol's wanting me to move in now.'

'Well, just you tell Mr. Nicol that you'll start with him now, and that you're getting married next year.'

Geordie moved to put an arm around her, but she shrugged him off.

'I'm making no promises, mind. I just said to tell the man you're getting married next year. Now it's time I was away. Lizzie's coming in to see me on her way home.' She slipped from the wall, saying, 'There's a funny feeling in the air. We're surely in for a change of weather,' and they headed down the hill and towards Agnes's home.

Agnes's mother and Lizzie were chatting when they arrived. After saying 'Ta-ra' to Geordie at the door, Agnes went to the window and watched him as he walked jauntily away.

'He's not gone back to the sea, then?' Lizzie asked.

'Oh he wanted to, right enough,' said Agnes, her voice unusually soft. 'But there'll be no sea for my Geordie. He'll be safer on land.' Her voice changed to its usual briskness when she asked, 'You've not had a cup of tea yet?' And she turned to fill the teapot from the kettle hanging over the fire.

'I'll leave you two to chat,' said the older woman as she moved away. 'I have work to do.'

Agnes sat down at the table beside her friend, arms folded. 'And how did you hear about the new job, then?'

'Babbie-Ann told a neighbour at church, and she told Mam.'

'Well, seems like she's good for something after all.' Agnes sniffed.

'The woman I'm going to work for – Janet Gray, her name is – fairly made sure she knew all about me. Asked me everything under the sun. Would you believe she asked me if I could cook? I told her how I started – helping to feed the men at harvesting, and me only nine years old, standing on a box to reach the sink to peel potatoes.'

'That surely satisfied her. And what about the bairns?'

'Two boys at school and two little ones – twins. And she's big with another one on the way. The old granny lives nearby, and I'll be sleeping with her. The father's a fisherman – most of them are fishermen at Winfield. I start next week. But what's been happening here? How's Dolly's baby?'

'Ah, there's a story there. The rumour was that the gypsies had stolen it.' Agnes waited a moment for Lizzie's reaction. 'But you needn't worry. It's not true.' And she went on to tell what had really happened.

Agnes had taken a basket of washing up the hill, pleased that the basket was so much lighter these days, now that she had to carry it by herself. As she reached the drying green, she thought she heard a small mewling sound. She set the basket down and picked up a shirt. But the sound came again, this time a little louder, sounding almost like the cry of a baby. She dropped the shirt back into the basket and straightened up, standing with hands on hips. The sounds came again, this time lasting longer than before. They seemed to come from the wood. Moving towards the shadowed trees and peering her way toward the sounds, she came upon Dolly, the baby still in the crook of her arm. She guessed by the colour of the girl's face that Dolly was no longer alive but placed her hand on the girl's chest to check. Then, lifting the baby from its mother's arm, she went back down the hill.

When the minister was told of Dolly's death, he had gone striding off up the hill. A little later, Agnes held the kitchen door open as he came in carrying Dolly's slack body in his arms. He carried her past Agnes and up the stairs. As Agnes heard his footsteps returning, she turned to him as he said, 'I'll just hitch up the pony. If you get the baby, Agnes, we'll get her to her grandmother.'

At the cottage, as Mrs. Buchan cuddled the baby on her knee, Agnes told Mrs. Buchan of finding Dolly and the baby, and the minister explained that Dolly was now at the manse. Mrs. Buchan thanked them and said, in answer to the minister's question, that she would be all right by herself.

After they left, she dipped the corner of a cloth in milk and tried to get the baby to suck on it, but the baby had just turned its head away and cried pitifully. There was a tap at the door and Jean the tinker woman came in.

'Well, Mrs. Buchan, the minister just passed and stopped to tell me. So this'll be poor Dolly's bairn?'

Mrs. Buchan lifted heavy eyes to her visitor. 'You'd better sit down, and I'll tell you what I've told nobody else.' She waited until Jean had settled herself before continuing. 'I'm not Mrs. Buchan. Buchan is my own name, for I never married Dolly's father. When Dolly was born the way she was, I knew it was the Lord's punishment for having a bairn out of wedlock.' The child had quietened as she spoke. 'But oh, wasn't having Dolly punishment enough, without having to face more years of the same with this one?' The wailing started again.

'Now, now, Mrs. Buchan. The bairn looks all right to me. There's nothing wrong with her lungs, anyway.'

'Not like Dolly. Dolly made no sound when she was born.' Mrs. Buchan's head dropped forward, and she began to cry softly.

'Whether this one's right or not, I can see it's going to be a bit of a burden for you, being on your own and you with a living to make. My own daughter's bairn is just three weeks old, and there's milk enough to feed two and more.'

Mrs. Buchan raised her head as the gypsy asked, 'Would you want me to take the bairn?'

'Take the bairn? But for how long? How long would you take her for?'

'We'll be moving off soon, we'll be leaving here, but we'll be back next spring.'

Mrs. Buchan nodded slowly. 'As you said, I have a living

to make.' She laid a hand on her visitor's arm. 'God bless you, Jean.'

Jean left with the baby, still wrapped in the little shawl.

The following evening, Mrs. Buchan found herself on the way to the hollow where the gypsies were camped. The smell of wood-smoke drifted towards her as she crouched low above the hollow, looking down on the circle of caravans and tents. A tall man, seated a little distance from the open fire, was speaking to the people sitting around him. The shadows of his long arms moved slowly this way and that as he told his story.

Mrs. Buchan looked beyond him to the caravan behind. Sitting on the top step was a dark-haired woman. The baby that fed at her breast was wrapped in the shawl. A child strayed from the firelight, and the story-teller's voice became louder. Whatever words he had woven into his tale, the child ran back to hide in its mother's skirts.

A dog barked and Mrs. Buchan, satisfied, turned for home.

– 12 –

Winfield

The sun was still bright on the horizon, sparkling across the wide sea and lighting the sandy cove below the cliffs. Fishing boats crunched on the shingle as men and women, ignoring the screaming gulls that flew down and away again, hauled the boats in rhythmical pulls from the water and up onto the sand near the rocks. Then came the division of the catch. Each fisherman had his share and, as was the custom, a share was set aside for the widow Mrs. Dunnar and her son Johnny. They would have this share of the catch until she remarried, or her son was old enough to fish.

It had been a good catch, and both men and women carried the baskets of fish up the path to the village. They drew near to where Lizzie stood with the twins. The two children were squatted down, pulling at the golden petals of some dandelions. Someone called out, 'Aye, aye, lass,' and Lizzie looked up to see a smiling young man – one of the few men who had no beard.

'That one's too little for you yet, Davie,' joked the man behind him. 'Better throw her back till she's grown a bit.'

The twins wailed in protest as Lizzie grabbed each one by the hand and, head held high, turned away from the men and towards the cottage.

'And was there much of a catch today?' Janet asked.

'Aye, not bad.' Lizzie busied herself with the children. 'There was a younger lad with them I hadn't seen before.'

'That'll be Davie – Fiddlin' Davie, they call him. Best keep away from that one.' She chuckled. 'He's got enough girls after him as it is.'

Lizzie felt her face grow hot. 'Time you two were in bed,' she chided the children, and Janet chuckled again.

It was late by the time Lizzie had finished her work. In the soft night air, she walked the path that fronted the cottages. One of those with a light still burning was where her cousin Freda lived, and Lizzie caught a glimpse of Freda sitting at the table with husband Matty. Baby Dorothy would be asleep in her cradle by now. Lizzie walked on to the last cottage in the row, which faced the path at an angle to the others. Inside, Janet's mother-in-law sat knitting in the dying light, her metal needles clicking quickly and surely.

'That you, Lizzie?'

Lizzie smiled, thinking *Who else would it be?* But the same question was asked every night.

'Was there a good catch this day?'

'Aye, Mrs. Gray. They didn't do badly.' Lizzie lit the paraffin lamp and set it on the table.

'Come and make yourself a cuppie tea before you go to bed. An' I'll have one with you.' This, too, was part of the routine.

The tea was made and, after the old woman had placed her knitting carefully on the smaller table by her side, Lizzie put a cup in her hands.

'That's a bonny bit of knitting.' Lizzie marvelled at how this blind woman managed the often complicated patterns.

'Ah well,' said Mrs. Gray, 'it takes in a little money when it's sold in Aberdeen, and men will aye need stockings. Now, do you know of that odd couple that stay on the croft not far from the kirk – name of Thomson?'

'Aye. They used to visit the minister and his wife when I worked there.'

'I heard that they are always on the take. You know, they've been here more than a dozen years now, and nobody yet knows where they came from nor why they settled here. I hear that Mr. Thomson's not able to work the farm on his own, and that they cannot get help. Janet saw the pair of them yesterday on the road to Hatton. You would think that they were always on the way to a funeral, always in those black clothes, the two of them.' She put her hands on the sides of her chair and stood up. 'Well, lass, you'll be needing your bed now, and I'm needing mine.'

In the bedroom, Mrs. Gray took off the white mobcap that covered her hair, before getting undressed and into her nightgown, and climbing into bed. The girl got ready for bed and lay down beside Mrs. Gray. She waited until the old lady's breathing became slow and regular, then crept out from between the sheets and over to the low window, where she knelt on the floor. The quiet sea glittered under a full moon.

'What ails you, Lizzie?'

Lizzie turned from the window and climbed back into bed.

'The sea's quiet tonight,' said the woman. 'You're lucky you weren't here last year. There was snow on the hills inland, and a terrible storm went right down the coast – in the month of June, would you believe? I'd felt it coming, so the men were warned and had the boats pulled well up before the storm came. One poor lad – just fourteen he was, same age as yourself – lost his life along with the rest of the crew, from a boat that had set out from Aberdeen.'

With the story of the shipwreck, Lizzie had forgotten her daydreaming, and was soon asleep.

– 13 –

Cruden Bay

Lizzie's day started as usual. After giving Mrs. Gray her tea in bed, she set off along the path to Janet's cottage, where she gave the boys their breakfast and got them off to school. Then the house was tidied and beds made.

Janet Gray watched as Lizzie moved between sink and shelves, clearing away the last of the dishes as the twins squabbled over a small wooden toy. Janet had tried Lizzie at baiting the lines, but the girl had hooked her fingers more often than the bait and spoiled the mussels in the process.

'Lizzie, there's a jumper here from my mother for my sister Minnie's boy. You could maybe walk over the sands to Cruden Bay with it and take Betty along with you.'

Lizzie, enjoying the thought of the visit and a change from routine, finished her work, took Betty by the hand and set off on the road above the cove. A little way along, they slipped down a sandy path and onto the beach that would take them to a shallow stream. Arriving at the stream, they waded across, then walked the short distance down the village road to Minnie's cottage.

By the time they were ready to return, the haar – a sea fog – was coming in, so Lizzie decided to return by way of the dunes.

They passed what looked like a well, but Lizzie, knowing how quickly a haar could surround them and hide the path home, hurried on.

They soon arrived at the village where, outside their cottage, Mrs. Dewar and her son Connon were baiting lines.

'Hello, Mrs. Dewar. Hello, Conn. We're just back from Cruden Bay. There's a fair haar out there today,' she said, with a tip of her head towards the sea.

Connon flicked his hair back from his dreamy eyes and bent his head to the lines again. 'Aye, but we didn't get lost in it. Got the boat in all right.'

Lizzie smiled and walked on with Betty to Janet's cottage, where Janet served up the midday meal. As they sat eating the broth and oatcakes, Lizzie spoke of their morning, how they had waded across the stream that fronted the village of Cruden Bay, then washed the sand from their feet at the village pump.

'Minnie said to say thank you for the jumper.' She paused. 'And Janet, on the way back I saw a boy standing right at the top of the dunes, but he ran off when he saw us.'

'That would have been poor Johnny Dunnar. He doesn't speak. Been like that for a few years now.'

'But what happened to him?'

Janet shook her head. 'We don't talk about it.' She stood up. 'We'd better get on with the baiting now, if your hands can take any more.' And she led the way to the bench outside.

That night, as Mrs. Gray sat knitting, she called out, 'That you, Lizzie?'

They chatted as Lizzie made their bedtime tea. Mrs. Gray told her that she hadn't been out that day. 'The rheumatics have been playing up. It's always the same when there's haar about. Who was out baiting the lines?'

Lizzie told her, mentioning Mrs. Dewar and her son.

'Don't be setting your cap at Conn, now,' Mrs. Gray warned. 'Not unless you want to travel far across the water.'

'Is he going away then?'

'Not that I've heard. But mark my words, he will... he will.'

The Drink

The following evening Lizzie had got the children off to bed. In the kitchen the smell of boiled cod lingered from the making of hairy tatties – a mix of boiled cod and potatoes. Lizzie was tidying up when the sound of a high-pitched voice came from the house behind. She had heard it before, but not this loud. The voice grew clearer as the woman came out of her house.

'I'll kill you, you little brats, sure's death I will!'

'That's Nan Greel having one of her turns,' said Janet. 'She'll be all right in a minute.'

But later, as Lizzie was leaving, she heard the raised voice again. She paused with her hand on the latch, head tipped to one side.

'Oh, she does her best with those two boys,' Janet went on, 'and them with a father like Stewie. There's hardly a penny he makes but it goes over his throat in drink. If he keeps going the way he's going now, I doubt if he'll ever scratch an old head.'

'And is there nothing she can do?'

'There's little can be done. His father, Airchie, was the same.' Janet gave a soft chuckle. 'There was one time Airchie and his pal, Fleet Munro, went into Aberdeen. They'd had a good catch and spent most of the money they'd made in the pub. They got lost on the way back to the horse and cart they'd come in and landed up weaving along the Castlegate. Three street-walkers saw the state they were in and came and put their arms round the men, dipping into their pockets while they cuddled. When Airchie realised what they were up to, well, he gave a roar like a bull. Along comes two bobbies, and when the street-walkers saw them, they started having a great carry-on about how the men had had their pleasure, and now wouldn't pay them. I wouldn't care, but for all Airchie liked the drink, he would no more have looked at any other woman than Mary, than he would fly in the fair air. Anyhow, at the end of it all, Airchie and Fleet landed up in the jail for the night. When he got home the next day, Airchie had to put up with a sore head and his wife's tongue as well.'

They both laughed at this.

'You would have thought that the like of that would have put him off drinking, but devil the chance. Airchie died young and his wife was left to bring up the bairns herself.' She sighed. 'You had better away now, before my mother starts wondering where you've got to.'

Lizzie and Mrs. Gray sat in their usual chairs, one each side of the fireplace, Mrs. Gray's hands busy as ever with her needles.

'Well, and what have you been up to today?'

'Oh, just the usual.'

But later, as they drank their tea, Lizzie told her of Nan Greel.

'Aye, it's a terrible thing, the drink. The temperance folk

came round not so long ago and between them and the wives, they got a few of the men off the drink. But there'll aye be one or two that just go on the same as ever. Right enough the men have hard lives but so have the women, what with having the children to look after besides everything else.' She paused for a moment and rested her knitting on her lap before going on. 'Mind you, even the women have it a bit easier nowadays than my mother and her like did. In those days, before the coming of rubber, all boots were made from leather. My mother would take my father on her back and walk into the sea and out to the boat, to keep his feet dry. There was no parish relief, nor any other kind of help in those days, if anything happened to your man.' And she picked up her knitting again.

'Agnes says she's not going to let Geordie go to the fishing,' said Lizzie. 'She's too frightened that anything will happen to him – says there's too many men lost at sea.'

'Well, that's up to her, but there's none of us know what's before of us.'

'But her sister Carrie's marrying a fisherman.'

'That'll be Willie Black. I heard about him from Janet. The Blacks are a lucky family. None of their men have been lost to the sea this long while back. And what about Agnes herself? Have they set the date yet?'

'They're talking about sometime at the end of summer.'

'Aye, that'll be a good time. Well, lass, speaking about time, it's time for my bed and yours as well, when you've to be up so early.'

– 15 –

Baiting and Birthing

It was early morning at Winfield as the men started back to shore after setting their baited lines at the fishing grounds. Lizzie was already on the bench outside the Grays' house, trying once more to bait hooks. Betty stood beside her watching, while twin Dorry went back and forth on the footpath, hopping and skipping. Lizzie was sucking on a bleeding finger when Andy passed her and went into the house. Conn, pausing on his own doorstep, noticed the girl, with the line she was working on lying on her lap. He walked slowly to where she sat and joined her on the bench.

'You see, Lizzie, it's easy enough once you know how, but you're likely going a bit fast. When you're learning, it's better to start slow.' He picked up a line. 'Now start again, and do what I do.'

And so he showed her, slowly, and she followed the movement of his fingers on her own line. Soon, she was baiting the hooks and managing to avoid the barbs.

'Now, just stay at that pace, till you're comfortable with it. Best be slow and right, than fast and wrong.'

He watched her for a little while before saying, 'I'll be away then,' leaving her relaxed and concentrating.

The two boys joined her. At twelve, Drew was a steady worker at the baiting. Jamie, two years younger, still had a way to go before he caught up. A little later, there came the sound of slow footsteps from the open door of the house, and Lizzie looked round to see young Mrs. Gray holding on to the doorpost with one hand. After a moment, she eased herself down onto the bench and picked up a line. But the size of her belly made it impossible to hold the line on her lap. She leaned back against the house wall and sighed.

'I doubt I'm much use just now,' she said.

'Conn's been helping me, Mrs. Gray, and I'll maybe be getting up some speed soon,' said Lizzie. 'Would you not be better to go inside and take it easy for a while?'

'Aye, maybe you're right.' Mrs. Gray raised herself awkwardly and went inside.

As the sun rose, Lizzie realised it was time to go indoors herself and prepare breakfast. Janet sat in an armchair by the grate. Lizzie soon had the children gathered round the table eating their porridge. Without warning, Dorry slapped her spoon down into her plate and spattered Jamie with porridge and milk. Jamie yelled. Lizzie took him to the sink and wiped him down.

'Get away to school now, boys. Here's your pieces for your dinner,' she said, handing each of them a wrapped sandwich. As they left she was berating Dorry for being 'a coarse girl, when you know your mother's none too well just now.' Then, to Mrs. Gray, she asked, 'Would you not take a wee lie down?'

'It seems awful lazy-like, but you know, Lizzie, I think I will.'

Once the woman had pulled herself slowly upstairs, and the kitchen table had been cleared, Lizzie returned to the bench outside. As the girls played with broken fish boxes, Lizzie began to get a feel for the baiting, and silently thanked Conn. She had only been working on the line for a short while when she thought she heard a sound.

'Hush, Dorry,' said Lizzie, but Dorry went on with her tuneless singing. 'Will you hush for a minute!'

This time she was sure. Someone was calling her name, but so softly that she couldn't tell, for a moment, where it came from.

'Oh my gweed, it's your mother.'

She grabbed each of the children by the hand and hurried them inside and up the narrow stairs. Janet lay on the bed, eyes closed.

'Put the twins in the bedroom.'

Lizzie took the children to their bedroom, sat them on the bed with a warning that they were to stay there, and returned to Janet.

'There's newspapers below the bed. Put them under me.'

Janet rolled over awkwardly, and Lizzie spread the papers thickly on the sheet. As she helped the woman to roll back, a gush of warm liquid splashed her arm.

'Now, if you'll just get the towels out of the little cupboard, and there's a basin over there.'

As Lizzie reached for the pile of clean, threadbare towels,

a groan came from Janet. She had drawn up her knees, and blood was oozing onto the papers. Lizzie returned to the bedside and was appalled to see a large bloody mass appear. She covered the afterbirth with one of the towels and tried not to retch as Janet strained to push the baby out.

'Janet? Janet!' a voice roared from downstairs.

'Up here, Andy!' Lizzie called and as he entered, she pointed to the bloody cord. Dorry appeared at the bedroom door.

'Lizzie,' said Andy, 'take the twins over to Meggie Jean's and bring her back here with you.'

When they returned, Lizzie took the twins off to their bedroom again.

'What is it?' asked Betty. 'What's wrong with Mam?'

'Oh, nothing you need bother your head about,' said Lizzie, and she drew the children into a finger-counting game.

It seemed a long time before Meggie Jean joined them. Taking Lizzie aside, she told her of the breech birth and the dead baby, and how she'd bound Janet's breasts to stop the milk.

'So she's all washed and tidied now, but she's very tired. There'll be extra work for you, lass, for Janet'll have to rest for a while – a few days at the least.'

Lizzie would sleep on a makeshift bed in the children's room that night, and for some nights to come.

– 16 –

Collieston

A few weeks later, Lizzie was sleeping in a different house. It had been decided that something about the house at Winfield – or about the village itself – had brought the bad luck that had made Janet lose her baby. Just along the coast, the harbour at Collieston was more accessible than the one at Winfield, and Andy had been pleased to move the family there. The bigger houses had been built along the top of the hill, facing the sea. The smaller cottages tumbled down in small groups, either side of the hill, almost to the harbour.

Outside one of the cottages, Janet and Lizzie sat baiting the lines. Old Mrs. Gray sat with them, knitting. Although the sun shone, there was a haar out over the sea.

'You've fairly come on at the baiting,' said Janet. 'You'll soon be as quick as the rest of us.'

Lizzie smiled. 'Well, I get plenty practice.'

Mrs. Gray cocked her head to one side and, with a slight frown, asked, 'Is there somebody coming?'

'Why, it's Big Annie with her bairns,' said Janet.

Annie, followed by her two children, ambled towards them and stopped by Mrs. Gray.

'Aye, aye, Mrs. Gray. Still keeping well?'

'As well as the good Lord allows,' was the reply. 'And how are you yourself? We haven't seen much of you this last while.'

'Och, the new minister's not like the old one. He never seems to have anything to spare, so Tommy's taken on work at the Thomsons.'

She plumped herself down beside Mrs. Gray and leant back against the cottage wall.

'Away and play with the twins,' she told her children. 'Well, and what's new? You don't hear much away up at that so-called farm.'

'Not a lot,' offered Janet. 'The fishing's been good, so Agnes's sister Carrie and her lad Willie are hoping to put a bit by, so's they can get wed at the end of summer.'

She glanced over to where the children were playing with the usual assortment of broken fish boxes and driftwood.

'Kirsty's fairly growing, Annie. How old is she now?'

'She'll be twelve on her birthday,' Annie said, frowning. 'But she's a handful, I can tell you.'

'And little Colin. He's coming on, too.'

'Can't believe it myself, but he's nearly six.' She smiled. 'Of course, he'll always be the baby. He's got a bit of a sore throat, so I thought I'd keep him off school today, and Kirsty as well, to keep him company.'

'Kirsty!' Mrs. Gray called. 'Come and see me a minute.'

Kirsty came and stood in front of the old woman. 'No, closer, Kirsty.'

She reached out a hand and smoothed it over the child's head and down her long hair.

'My, what lovely hair you have, Kirsty, and I know you're a bonny lass too. How do you like the school?'

'I like it fine,' Kirsty replied, looking at the ground.

'And you're good at your lessons?'

'The teacher says that I am.'

Here her mother interrupted with 'Aye, well, that's enough. Now g'way and play with the rest of them. And you, Mrs. Gray, you'll maybe miss being in your own house?'

'Not a bit of it. I have my own room here, and I can be with the family when I've a mind to. It could be lonesome at times in my own house, you know, even though folk were good to me. But they have their own lives to lead, and busy ones at that.'

'That's true. I've knocked at Mrs. Buchan's door more than once, and she's been out with her creel, more often than not,' said Annie. 'And tell me, has there been any more word about Connon going to America?' She shivered, and without waiting for a reply, went on, 'That haar's creeping in again. I suppose I'd better be getting back. He'll be wanting his meal when he comes in.'

'Lizzie,' said Janet, 'why don't you take the twins and walk a bit of the way with them?'

Annie and Lizzie walked together as the children ran on ahead, their voices coming back to the two women.

Lizzie smiled. 'My, but they can chatter, can't they!' Then, seriously, she said, 'Not like that poor Johnny Dunnar. I see him now and again, and always on his own. Does he not speak at all?'

'Oh, you'll not know the story then?' said Annie. And she went on to tell Lizzie what had happened.

The four boys, Hamish Ogilvie and his little brother Ewan, with Jake Cowie and Johnny Dunnar, had set off for the beach. When they came to the cave mouth that they'd been warned against entering 'or you'll be drowned', Jake had dared Johnny to go in with him, taunting him with 'how can anyone be drowned when the tide is out?'

The two boys entered the dripping cave, watched by Hamish. Little Ewan went to follow but was warned by his brother to stay where he was. As they stood at the entrance, they heard the sound of the boys' voices echoing inside, and their laughter. There followed a short confusion of their voices, a loud splash, then silence. Hamish stood with his hand against the warm rock outside in the bright sunlight and peered into the cave but could see nothing. He called the boys' names but heard only his own voice echoing away into the darkness. It seemed a long time before he heard the erratic, squelching footsteps and Johnny, white-faced, appeared before him.

'Where's Jake?' Hamish asked. 'Is he drowned?'

Johnny nodded.

'Did you drown him? Did you push him in? I heard you laughing,' he accused. 'I'm going to tell. C'mon, Ewan.' And they ran off, scrambling up the rocks towards the village.

'Well,' Annie continued, 'it would seem that Johnny had pushed him in, whether by accident or not, but whatever happened he hasn't spoken a word from that day to this. Oh, they tried everything – took him to the doctor, even doused him in St. Olaf's well, the holy well that kept the cholera from these parts years ago, when it was raging all around.'

'I thought I saw a well when we were coming back over the dunes from Cruden Bay,' Lizzie interrupted.

'Then you wouldn't have seen the inscription,' Annie continued, 'St. Olaf's well, low by the sea, where pest nor plague shall never be.' Anyhow, nothing worked. Mrs. Dunnar was heart-broken. Her only bairn not being able to speak, and everybody saying he was a murderer. And of course there could be no schooling for him, though she tries hard to school him at home.' She gave a sigh. 'But what's the use of that? Where would a lad that cannot speak find work?'

'And what about the Cowies?'

'Well, they didn't want to go on living here after losing their boy like that, and him the youngest. Last I heard they were living in Peterhead.'

'I'd better be turning back now, Annie. I'll see you the next time you're by.'

As she hurried the children along, Lizzie felt the chill coming in from the sea. The haar was creeping towards them, and there seemed to be a faint booming in the distance.

Back at the cottage, she was helping Janet take in the last of the baskets and lines when the boys came home from school.

'I fear there's a storm coming up, Lizzie. It crossed my mind last night when we had the full moon.' Lizzie looked puzzled. 'Aye, the moon is mistress of the tides, but you'll learn about that.'

As they stacked the baskets of baited lines in the little lean-to behind the house, Lizzie said, 'I wonder how far out the men are?'

'Best not to think of it,' said Janet. 'You'll learn to do that as well.'

Once inside, Lizzie hung the pot of broth over the fire. The wind had risen and, within moments, was shrieking round the house. As they sat down to eat, Janet chivvied the boys to stop larking about. To the wide-eyed twins she said, 'Come on, girls. You've heard a storm before. Eat your soup.'

Later, as the boys sat with their homework, Mrs. Gray at her knitting, and Janet repairing trousers, Lizzie took up a pair of knitting needles and some wool. 'Now, Betty and Dorry, if you'll get out the needles and your knitting, I'll show you how to do the next bit.'

She had been teaching the girls to knit and had been surprised how Dorry was picking it up quite quickly, while Betty seemed not to be interested. Tonight, as the wind howled around the house, Lizzie was glad that she had the twins and the knitting to occupy her.

When the door burst open, she started. Andy was almost blown in, then had to use his full weight against the door to close it again. Janet busied herself setting a place for him at the table while he went to change his sodden clothes. He returned in dry clothes and had eaten before Janet asked, 'All safe?'

'Aye, all safe.'

– 17 –

The Wedding

The breeze ruffled Johnny Dunnar's hair as he stood high on the hill that overlooked the path leading to the village. A stream of people passed below him. At the head of the line were the newly-married couple and behind them, dressed in 'Sunday best', came the guests. The hats adorned with flowers and ribbons worn by the women gave the scene a festive air. Some of the children walked sedately with their parents, but most ran back and forth. As the crowd disappeared into the large barn that stood behind the houses, Johnny ran back down the far side of the hill.

Inside the barn the people spread out, finding seats at the tables that had been pushed together to form one long table. An odd assortment of plates were heaped with food. Lizzie found herself next to Conn, and they chatted companionably while they ate. There was much chatter and merriment from the guests, and now and then a burst of laughter from those nearest the bride and groom, the effect of some ribald humour. Willie, the groom, would sometimes join in the laughter while Carrie, now Mrs. Black, would either shake her head and smile, or turn her head away to hide her blushes.

Feasting over, the women cleared the tables, leaving some

of the food on a table at the side for later. Bottles of whisky and jugs of ale stood on another table. Willing hands lifted tables and chairs to the walls as the musicians made their way to the far end of the barn. Robbie Taylor carried his mouth organ and Davie Phillips his fiddle. Daniel limped over with his own fiddle, while Conn went to stand beside him with his melodeon. Lizzie helped Mrs. Gray to a seat, where they were joined by Janet. There were some discordant notes while the band tuned up before they struck up a reel. Andy extended a hand to Janet, who shook her head and nodded towards Lizzie. Lizzie and Andy joined a set of dancers where one hefty lad, his right arm linked through that of his partner's, spun her round until her feet lifted from the floor, to delighted yells and applause. At the end of the dance, Andy and Lizzie caught up with Geordie and Agnes as they returned to their seats.

'Well, Geordie, you'll have heard that Conn's leaving us. How about joining Robbie and me on the boat?' asked Andy.

Geordie smiled, but before he could answer he felt Agnes's grip on his arm and the smile died.

'Sorry, Andy. It's the land for me.'

'Ah well.' Andy shrugged and moved away with Lizzie. They passed Drewie and Jamie standing at the side table, stuffing their mouths with food. Andy laughed.

'That two'll be sick before morning!'

While the musicians took a break, Conn moved through the crowd and crossed the floor to speak to Lizzie.

'Will you come out for a breath of fresh air?'

They wended their way between the children, who were

doing their own mock dancing near the door. A small collie dog wandered in as they left. Outside, Lizzie breathed deeply of the cool sea air. The light of a golden harvest moon spilled across the quiet sea and over the boats below them, each partially silhouetted by its own black shadow. They started walking slowly down the hill.

'You know I changed my mind about America and that I'll be going to New Zealand soon, with Willie and Carrie?'

Lizzie nodded, her eyes on the path as she walked ahead of him.

'I wondered, Lizzie, if you'd come with me.'

Lizzie stopped and looked up at him.

'Oh, we'd be married first, of course.'

'Conn, I'm not ready for marriage yet, and what would I be doing in a strange place away from all the folk I know?'

Conn sighed. 'Aye, I can see the sense in what you say. It's just that it would have been fine to have had your company.' The sound of fiddles striking up came to them. 'Will we just get back, then?'

The dancing had started again. Some of those who weren't dancing sat with their feet thumping the floor in time with the music. Mrs. Gray was clapping her hands rhythmically as Lizzie sat down.

'Look at Big Annie dancing,' said Janet. 'She's light on her feet, for all her size.'

The dance ended and, as the floor cleared, Robbie Taylor, his face sweating in the heat of the room and from the whisky he had taken, stood and announced loudly, 'And now while you get your breath back, we'll have a song from Margaret Brown.'

The dark-haired girl sang a song, sweet and clear, of unrequited love. During the applause that followed, Lizzie commented, 'She has a bonny voice, but that was real sad-like.'

Janet explained that the girl had been walking out with Davie Phillips. But Davie now had a new girlfriend – '*Another* new girlfriend,' she emphasised. 'No doubt she'll get her heart broken too. I'm thinking that his single days won't be over for a while yet.'

As the music started again, a small whine attracted Lizzie's attention. She looked over at the dog which had passed them earlier. It was swaying as it walked, then one leg seemed to give way altogether. Kirsty had noticed it too and went over to the animal. She guided it underneath one of the tables and crawled in after it.

But it wasn't long before Tommy noticed her absence and asked Annie where the girl was. Annie went off, grumbling, to look for her and finally saw Kirsty's feet poking out from under a table. Bending down awkwardly, she asked the girl what she was playing at, and to come out of there.

'They made the dog drunk, Mam,' Kirsty explained as she crawled out, 'and I was petting it.'

'What do you mean, made the dog drunk? You're not speaking sense.'

'I could smell it,' explained the girl as she stood up and, as Annie pulled her along the room, she added, 'But it's all right now. It's sleeping.'

It was early in the morning before the celebrations ended. The barn emptied as chatting groups made their way along the moonlit paths of Collieston. They would have little sleep before it was time to start the never-ending tasks once more.

– 18 –

A Song at Christmas

Some worthy had predicted a bad winter. 'But he's not aye right,' the people comforted themselves, and when the fine weather did break, it was blamed on bad luck – someone had not paid heed to one or other of the many superstitions. This afternoon, there was a lull in the constant wind and rain, and Lizzie's sister Jane took the chance to walk the cliff road from Winfield to Collieston, along with younger sister Margaret.

The farm that the family had lived on had been sold and, along with it, their tied cottage. They were now living at Winfield, where Lizzie's father had taken over Old Tom's carting work, transporting fish to the train that would carry them to markets in the south, and helping out on the surrounding farms.

Jane now brought the news that the family were all settled in at Winfield. Settling in did not take long, for they had few possessions. Now the twins sat on the wooden settle. Dorry, bored, swung her legs, her heels thumping rhythmically against the wooden front, but her legs stilled as Margaret came and sat between the two girls.

Lizzie prepared to scramble the eggs that Jane had brought. Cooked that way, they would go further. As she broke each egg, she crushed the shell in her hand before throwing it into the bin, following the belief that crushing the shell would save a fisherman from drowning. The eggs would be a welcome treat as they had had to use herring from the salt barrel for days now, while the fishing was so poor.

'So the men are out?' asked Jane.

'Aye. They'll be trying for crabs at this time of year,' commented Janet. 'It gives us a break from baiting the lines.'

Having eaten and cleared up, they gathered round the fire. Mrs. Gray picked up the jersey she was knitting in the usual dark blue wool. From memory, she used the complicated pattern which had been passed down the generations, to be worn only by local fishermen. Should a man's body be washed ashore many miles from his home, his jersey would identify the area from which he had come. Janet and Lizzie each took an article of clothing from the heaped basket of clothes for repairing.

'And how old are you now, Margaret?' asked Mrs. Gray.

'I'm twelve, Mrs. Gray.'

'So there's three years between Lizzie and yourself. We had a nice tea for Lizzie's birthday, didn't we, Lizzie?'

'Aye. We had bannocks* with syrup, and biscuits from the shop,' Lizzie said.

Janet turned to Jane. 'And we hear there might be a bigger celebration to come, now that you're walking out with Davie's brother George?' Before Jane could reply, Mrs. Gray

---

* oatcakes

commented on how she'd heard that Sandy was doing a good job on the Thomson farm, although the work was far too much for one man. Janet added that 'he surely didn't take after his sister, then.' Jane went on to talk of 'poor Nan Greel', and that she was glad to hear that her husband Stewie had taken an oath to stay off the drink when the temperance folk had last visited.

'Easy enough for him just now,' said Janet, 'when there's barely enough coming in to keep us in food, let alone drink.'

As she finished speaking, they heard the sound of the wind rising again. 'Time we were heading back,' said Jane. Dorry bewailed the parting as they donned jackets and went out into the darkening afternoon. Jane reached for her little sister's hand and, heads bent, they took off for the cliff path and their new home.

The women were busy on the days leading up to Hogmanay – the last day of the year. Houses were cleaned from top to bottom and, to prevent ill-luck, knitting was hurriedly finished. Any knitter who knew that a garment would not be completed by midnight would unravel the garment. The villagers celebrated Christmas under the old calendar, feasting on the fifth day of January. On that day, children would awake to find an orange or some other small luxury in the socks that they had hung up the night before. The men who had over-indulged at Hogmanay had now recovered enough to enjoy the feasting on the fifth. Throughout the day, the villagers visited friends, relations and neighbours. Lizzie went to her family at Winfield, taking the twins with her. Here, the adults enjoyed some homemade wine, and everyone enjoyed thick slices of currant cake. Lizzie sat beside her father, who soon took out his mouth organ and started to play softly. The music grew louder as he played a swinging reel, and some of the children got up and danced, returning to their seats as the music ended.

'Let's have a song, Lizzie,' called out one of the visiting fishermen.

Lizzie gave the name of her song to her father, and to his accompaniment she sang a sad lullaby. 'My Yellow-Haired Bairn' told the story of how the baby's father had been lost at sea. After the last note had died away, there was silence for a moment, then applause from the appreciative audience, for Lizzie had a fine voice. When the applause had quietened, Lizzie heard a low sobbing. She went over to the settle to comfort Dorry, who sat with tears running down her face.

'It's all right, Dorry. It's only a song.'

That night, as Lizzie was settling the children down to sleep, Dorry sat up, a frown on her face.

'Did the babby's dad never come back, Lizzie?'

'Oh aye. The big fishes pushed him up to the top of the water, and he got out onto the sands and walked back to his house. But he was awful wet when he got home! Now, lie down and sleep.'

As she left the room, she glanced back, and was pleased to see the smile on Dorry's face as she snuggled down.

– 19 –

Daisy

The villagers along the coast had many hard times to endure before the sound of the gypsies' return was heard. Jamie and Davie, who had climbed up one of the trees in the small wood, were the first to hear the faint tinkling in the distance. As the gypsies drew nearer, the tinkling grew louder until it changed to the sound of pots and pans clanging lightly against the sides of the leading caravan. The string of horse-drawn carts and caravans came round a bend in the path and passed beneath the boys, who watched until they disappeared over the next hill. Soon, a column of smoke drifted up from the hollow where they had set up camp. While the men were occupied with the feeding and watering of the horses, the women busied themselves preparing a meal. Boys worked alongside the men, girls with the women.

The following evening, Mrs. Buchan sat before her small fire. She knew the gypsies were back, and tensed as she heard the expected knock on the door. Jean stood there, holding the little girl's hand.

Mrs. Buchan settled them by the fire and brought tea for Jean. As she handed her granddaughter a small mug of milk, she looked at her closely for the first time. There was only a trace of her mother in the pretty face. She sat quietly while the two adults chatted.

'Go and see the dolly,' said Jean, pointing to the cradle.

The child put her mug down carefully and trotted across the room. As she looked into the cot, Mrs. Buchan heard the words she had dreaded.

'Dolly, dolly.' The little girl turned and looked at Jean. 'Jean. Dolly 'n' a bed.' Jean saw Mrs. Buchan fight back the tears as she asked, 'Nice dolly, Daisy?'

'Yes. Nice dolly,' the child replied.

'We've called her Daisy,' said Jean. 'But she's young enough to get used to another name if you wanted to change it.'

'No. It's a bonny name for a bonny lass.' Mrs. Buchan smiled.

'So you'll manage to have her back?'

'She'll be the daughter I never had.'

Later, as the gypsy went to leave, Daisy started to follow her to the door.

'No, no, Daisy. You bide with the lady. Her name is Gran.'

Accustomed as she was to staying with any one of the gypsy families, Daisy turned back quite happily to the cot.

'Oh, and there's this,' said Jean. And she took from her large bag a cloth which she handed to Mrs. Buchan. The older woman once more had to fight back the tears as she looked at the still-bright knitted shawl – the shawl that had once wrapped her daughter's doll then, later, her daughter's baby. She stood up and put an arm round the younger woman and walked her to the door. The gypsy smiled her goodbye as she left.

That night, as her grandmother got Daisy ready for bed, she saw the birthmark on her forearm, and knew her to be Daniel's child. There was no mistaking the red birch-leaf.

For the first few days with her granddaughter, Mrs. Buchan took Daisy with her on her visits to the surrounding farms, and the smiling child became quite a favourite. But she slowed Mrs. Buchan down and was too heavy to carry in her arms for long. One bright spring morning, one of the fishermen had dropped in with a load of fish. He went off after giving Daisy a pretty shell and a cheery smile.

Mrs. Buchan had started to place the firm, fresh fish into her creel when she noticed the small sheet of tarpaulin that the fisherman had thrown carelessly aside. After washing the sheet and putting it outside to dry, she put more fish into the creel, leaving some space on top. The tarpaulin dried quickly. Mrs. Buchan brought it in and placed it over the fish in the creel, tucking it down the sides. Next she cut two long strips from a piece of cloth, tied the ends of each one low on the straps of the creel, and placed the creel on a chair.

'Well, Daisy, let's see how you like this.' She smiled as she sat Daisy into the creel.

The loose ends of the strips were tied round Daisy's waist. Mrs. Buchan then turned her back to the chair, stepped backwards towards it and, slipping her arms into the straps, got the creel onto her back and moved off. After the child's initial surprise at finding herself aloft, her grandmother heard her giggling with delight.

They set off for the Nicols' farm. As they neared it, Mrs.

Buchan skirted the fields of other houses. She kept walking until she found the gap in the low wall that led into the Nicols' place. Mrs. Nicol, outside hanging up washing, saw the pair and smiled a welcome. As they reached her she said, 'Come away in, Mrs. Buchan. You'll have a cup of tea.' Daisy held her chubby arms out, and Mrs. Nicol lifted her down. She took the little girl's hand and led her into the house, while Mrs. Buchan left her creel outside in the cool shade of the wall.

Mrs. Buchan sat at the table with Daisy on her knee, and the two women chatted as Mrs. Nicol prepared a pot of tea and set out oatcakes and butter. She admired the fish that Mrs. Buchan had placed in the sink. 'My, but Mr. Nicol and the boys'll enjoy those.'

'And how are the boys, Mrs. Nicol?'

'Och, they're just fine. Willie's his dad over again, and just as interested in the farming. Alec's going the same way.' She paused for a moment, then continued, 'But Jockie now, the youngest, well, I'm not so sure. A fine lad, but he's not made his mind up if the farming's for him. Oh, he pulls his weight right enough, but I've the feeling that he'll take a different path.'

The two guests finished their tea and Mrs. Nicol paid for the fish. There was no problem this time in getting Daisy back on top of the creel, and she waved back at Mrs. Nicol before they set off again.

Johnny

Spring had passed with few of the wild storms that usually came at that time of year, and soon it was time for the annual migration of villagers. Boats belonging to those who had gone for the herring fishing lay high on the beach. The men would follow the shoals far down the coast in boats other than their own. Many of the women would also go south, gutting and filleting the fish as it was brought ashore, before being packed and transported to destinations in Britain, and to places as far away as Russia. The boats of the fishermen who were not following the herring were also idle today, for it was Sunday. No-one fished on a Sunday. Once that was for religious reasons. Now, it was against the law.

Some of the houses that now lay empty had been rented out as holiday accommodation. The villagers who had stayed behind and moved from their homes into outhouses and sheds would 'look after' the houses, from where the holiday-ing townsfolk who now peopled the streets would sally forth. They would take their children to enjoy the sea air and the natural attractions of the harbour or visit the towns to the north – Peterhead, or as far as Fraserburgh.

One of those remaining in the village was Mrs. Dunnar.

She saw little of Johnny, who often disappeared to walk long distances along the coast roads. This bright day she had come to the door of her house on hearing her name called. Robbie stood outside with his arm round Johnny's shoulders. As they neared, she saw her son purse his lips together, frowning, and make a short humming sound. The sound became 'Mmm' then 'Muh'. She watched him struggle. Then, finally, 'Mam'.

Later, they sat by the empty grate, the young boy happily crunching on some oatcakes, while Robbie told Mrs. Dunnar what had happened.

Johnny had gone wandering along the beach, alone as usual, and had come upon some of the boys from the village, amongst them Drewie and his brother Jamie. Johnny made to turn back as one of the bigger boys shouted, 'There's Johnny Dunnar. Let's get hold of him.' The speaker and another older boy had rushed forward, taking hold of Johnny's arms. Cheered on by a third boy, he was pulled towards the high rocks which were set back from the beach. They stopped at a cave entrance and taunted him.

'This is where you drowned Jake, isn't it?' said one. Another added, 'Aye, little wonder you can't speak, for what would you have to say? And how would you like to go in there again, eh, Johnny Dunnar?' One of the boys who held him nodded his head towards the rock face. Both boys now threw him forward and he almost fell into the cave.

The young lad put out a hand to steady himself in the narrow passage but withdrew it quickly as a sharp edge bit. He stumbled as he went forward then, half sliding over the slimy wetness, the darkness closed around him. Now he stopped, listening to the water dripping into pools with metallic, echoing sharpness.

As he went forward again and turned a corner, the smell of fresh salt air changed to that of a damp mustiness. Further on, the scuttling and clicking of live things grew fainter, then ceased. His eyes were becoming accustomed to the gloom and, by the dim light that filtered down from a spout-hole above, Johnny could see that he was approaching the pool – the same pool that Jake had walked towards, ahead of Johnny, on that fateful day. And Johnny remembered. He remembered their nervous laughter of bravado, how Jake had slipped suddenly from Johnny's sight. He remembered how his friend had bobbed back to the surface, Johnny reaching his hand down as the boy sunk back again, and the bubbles rising as he called his friend's name again and again. He must get help! Then the rush to get back out, feet sliding every which way, falling more than once. When he finally appeared at the cave's entrance, it was to stand, mouthing and silent, while he was accused of drowning his friend.

When they saw what the boys were doing to Johnny, Drewie and Jamie had run off for help. They met Robbie, and the three of them had hurried back to the beach. Robbie, taking long strides down the hill, heard the shouting, loud and repetitive, coming from the boys standing before the cave. As he got nearer, he recognised them now as the two Greel brothers and 'Borsie' Flint. Borsie held a little back from the two, who shouted 'Who killed Jake?' over and over again. The chant turned to almost hysterical laughter, and they fell about, thumping each other in wild delight. Robbie went to Johnny, who still stood by the cave mouth. 'Are you all right, lad?' The boy opened his mouth, took a deep breath and 'Aye,' he said. It came out softly, but Robbie heard the word. 'Come on, then.'

As he walked away with Johnny, Drewie and Jamie following, he called back to the trio, now sobered, 'We'll see to you lot later.'

Mrs. Dunnar wiped her eyes once more on the corner of her apron.

'Will you have a drop more tea, Robbie?'

'No, no, Mrs. Dunnar. I'd better be away now and see to those three young limmers.'

She walked him to the door. 'There's no way I can thank you, Robbie.'

Robbie looked a little embarrassed. 'Och, it was just lucky I was there before they got up to any more mischief,' he said, then turned away and set off down the road.

Agnes and Geordie

The sea lapped gently at Lizzie's bare feet as she walked slowly along the beach. She had taken the twins to their first day at the dames' school and had decided to walk back by way of the sands on this fine autumn day. Further along the beach a neighbour, old Mrs. Robertson, was examining something that she held in her hand. As Lizzie approached, Mrs. Robertson called, 'See what I've found.' She stood looking at a small ship's lantern and was wiping off the sand with an arthritic hand as she spoke. 'Hardly a scratch on it, and once I've cleaned it up, it'll be real bonny on my mantelpiece.' She turned to Lizzie. 'It's true what they say. You never know what the incoming tide will bring.' Lizzie admired the lantern as Mrs. Robertson asked, 'Well, you'll be looking forward to the wedding?' Agnes was to be married the following Saturday.

'Oh aye. We're all looking forward to it, and the twins are real excited, too. Their mam's had to make new dresses for them, they're growing at such a rate. Well, I'd better away and see to Mrs. Gray.'

The sound of Mrs. Robertson singing followed her as she climbed the hill. In a strong voice that wavered only slightly, she sang the old hymn, '*God is love, his mercy brightens all the paths in which we rove.*'

As she walked along the path in front of the cottages, Lizzie saw Mrs. Gray sitting outside a neighbour's house.

'It's clouding over,' Lizzie said.

'Aye, lass. I could feel it cooling a bit.' And turning to her neighbour she said, 'I think I'll just go in now.'

As she stood up holding her bag of knitting, Lizzie took the old lady's free arm and walked with her slowly to her cottage. Mrs. Gray's foot touched the herring barrel at the door, and she shook off the guiding hand.

'I'm fine now, lass,' she said and, independence restored, entered ahead of Lizzie. While the girl made tea, they, too, talked of Agnes's wedding. Many of the same people would be there as had been at Carrie's wedding. The same men would be playing their instruments. Only Conn would be missing. He had sailed, as Mrs. Gray had predicted, for Tasmania, with Carrie and Willie.

On the day of the wedding, Betty's shoes could not be found.

'If they're not found soon, you'll go to the church barefoot,' Lizzie threatened.

'Oh, they're here.' This from Dorry, as she straightened up from the settle, shoes in hand. Lizzie knew that Dorry had probably been up to her tricks again, but there was no time to tax her with it.

The children behaved well during the wedding service. They were accustomed to sitting quietly in church. But when they left, despite Lizzie's admonitions, they lagged behind as they set off for the hall in which the guests would feast and dance. By the time they got to the hall, guests were already seated.

Lizzie found places for them at a table near where the band would be playing. The players sat at the same table. The only unoccupied seats were between Fiddlin' Davie and Gerda, one of the fisher lasses. Lizzie sat the two girls next to Davie and took the one furthest from him. Davie went on eating, seeming not to notice their arrival, as Lizzie busied herself with the children. But later in the evening, just as the band had started another tune, she saw Davie place his fiddle on his seat and turn to walk towards where she sat. Looking up at the young man who stood beside her, tapping a foot to the music, she smiled at him. 'They play well, don't they?'

'Will you dance, then?' he asked.

They joined the dancers on the floor. A few minutes later she saw that Davie had found another partner. Then Lizzie caught sight of a familiar head of fair hair. It was Donald. He was dancing awkwardly with little Kirsty. Though Kirsty herself didn't look so 'little', thought Lizzie, as when she had last seen her.

She's really too young to have her hair up like that, she thought. The hair and the cut-down dress that she wore made her look far more mature than her years.

The evening passed quickly, and Lizzie enjoyed seeing and talking with people she hadn't seen for some time.

Later, leaving early with the twins, she was only a little surprised to pass Donald being held against the outside wall, with Kirsty's father's hands on his shoulders.

'So you just keep away from her, d'ye hear? She's only a bairn!'

Tommy removed his hands and returned to the hall as Donald slid drunkenly down the wall. Lizzie hurried the twins along. When she looked back he sat there still, his head fallen forward on his chest.

– 22 –

Smugglers

In Janet's house the peat fire warmed the room where many of the women, some with children, had gathered. Now that winter was here, there was little fishing, and they had some respite from the baiting of the lines. The women knitted and sewed, oblivious to the smoke and smell of the cruises – the boat-shaped lamps holding lit wicks, which were filled with fish oil. Someone commented that Agnes and Geordie were now settled at the Nicols' farm, Drydykes, following their wedding, and there was mention of Donald.

'And it wasn't just at the wedding that he was in a state,' said a voice from the corner of the room. 'I hear that he's taken to the drink.'

'Aye, and Tommy and Big Annie have been keeping Kirsty close to home since the wedding,' said another. 'Annie's brother Sandy's still working for the Thomsons, but it's too much for one man. It's maybe time they gave up that place before it falls into rack and ruin.' The speaker paused then added, 'But then, the land itself's worth quite a bit.'

Another of the women commented that she hadn't seen Big Annie for a while and was told that her little boy Colin had caught measles on a visit to Peterhead, and she had been spending her time cosseting him, well after the infection had gone.

'Ah well,' said Mrs. Gray. 'You'd expect that from Annie. But what about Mrs. Dunnar's boy? Wasn't that a blessing, Johnny being able to speak again, after all this time. What boys was that, that put him back in the cave?'

Mention was made of the Greel boys, and there were murmurs of agreement when someone said, 'Little wonder, with a father like they have. Nan Greel has her hands full, right enough.'

The door opened and was shut quickly against the cold air.

'My goodness, I never thought to see *you* tonight,' said Lizzie, as Jane moved away from the door. Lizzie gathered her skirts and edged along the settle, making room for her sister. As Jane rubbed her hands, she asked if they had heard about the drownings further up the coast. Three men had gone out on the swollen sea, and only one had returned. One of the women recognised the name McFarlane, and asked did Jane know which of the family had come back. Jane, frowning, told them she thought it was a young boy.

'Then it's the father and the older son who've been lost,' said one of the women. 'The three of them always fished together. Poor Bess McFarlane.'

There was a silence, each woman thinking not just of the McFarlanes, but of her own men.

'The fire's getting low,' said Janet. She got up and stirred the glowing peat, adding another peat before using the bellows. The flames brightened the room.

'There's some seaweed here, Lizzie, if you want to roast it for the bairns. I'll put the poker in to heat.'

Soon it was hot enough and, once she had roasted some of the seaweed with the poker, Lizzie was hard put to keep the children from burning their fingers. Led by Dorry, they tried to snatch at it before it had had time to cool.

'There's word that Old Tom's not getting any better,' said Jane.

They agreed amongst themselves that Tom had done well as 'after all, he won't see eighty again.'

And so they chatted on until Jane thought it was time she was getting back. Lizzie offered to walk part of the way and, amid calls of 'Goodnight' and 'Goodnight, then,' they donned their warm jackets and took off into the night.

The moonlight brightened their way along the cliff road, though they had to pause now and then as scattered clouds covered the moon and obscured the path.

They had walked for some time before Lizzie said, 'I'll just be turning back now,' and she stood and watched her sister walk away. When Jane reached a bend in the road, she turned round, and they waved to each other before Jane walked on and was hidden from view. Lizzie had started on her way home when she thought she heard the sound of a man's voice. Ahead of her she saw a man appear from her left who must have climbed from the beach. He was followed by a straggle of men in single file as they crossed the path ahead of her. The first man held a barrel on his shoulders. Some of the others also carried barrels, the rest held various boxes. A cloud passed over the moon and when it cleared Lizzie found herself alone on the path. She started to run and ran all the way back to the house.

The guests had all gone, and as she leaned back against the closed door, panting, Janet came down the stairs.

'Whatever's the matter, lass?' She took Lizzie's hands, drew her towards the fire and sat her down.

Lizzie sat quiet for a moment until her breathing had settled, then told her employer what she had seen.

'Ah,' said the older woman. 'You'll have seen the smugglers.' And she went on to tell Lizzie how rife smuggling had been in the old days. 'Though they don't show themselves to just anyone. Looks like you've got a touch of the second sight, Lizzie.' Lizzie's eyes widened. 'Now, lass, don't you worry. It'll bring you no harm. But never go looking for it either, for the second sight will come to you and leave you as it wills.'

Lizzie, now calm, slept with old Mrs. Gray that night as usual. She slept deeply and dreamlessly.

The Little Boat

Winter seemed to last forever, but gradually the air softened, and the skies cleared. One fine sunny morning Mrs. Buchan walked with Daisy up the hill, past the manse and through the trees to Daniel's cottage. Daniel invited them in and the three sat at the table. On the table lay a little wooden boat, at which he had been whittling.

'I'll come right to the point, Daniel,' said Mrs. Buchan. 'Daisy's getting too heavy for me to carry these days, and the walking's a bit much for her.' She paused for a moment. 'You'll know that she's yours?' Turning the child's arm gently, she showed Daniel the birthmark. He looked away for a moment, then down at the little girl beside him.

'I was thinking that maybe I could leave her with you when I'm out with the creel and come back for her on the way home. She's a good bairn and won't give you any trouble.'

Daisy had sat with her eyes on the boat while they spoke.

'Would you like to play with the boat?' Daniel asked her.

He pushed it towards her, and the little girl smiled and took it between her hands, turning it this way and that.

'So if you're willing, when will I leave her with you?'

'You'll be travelling with your creel today?' Mrs. Buchan

nodded. 'Then you can leave her with me now, if she'll stay.'

'Do you want to stay with Daniel, Daisy? I'll come back for you after.'

Daisy nodded. Mrs. Buchan swung her creel onto her back and made to leave. Before she stepped over the threshold, she looked back and said, 'Cheerio, then.'

'Cheerio,' replied Daisy, without looking up. Father and daughter sat with heads close together, engrossed in the little boat.

Janet had taken the twins to Fraserburgh to visit relatives for a few days, so Lizzie was free to help Mina Paterson with little Molly and the baby, Will. When not needed at the Patersons', she would join the women who were preparing the fish by splitting and cleaning them before putting them outside to dry. One day, when Mina didn't need her help and the women had put out the last of the fish, she went indoors to get washed and tidied up, then set off for Drydykes.

At the narrow road that led to the cottage, she could see Agnes at the door, waving across the field to where Geordie was working. Agnes smiled a welcome when she spotted Lizzie. Later, while they drank tea, Agnes pushed her chair back a little from the table.

'So, how long now, Agnes?'

'It should be July, though I'm big for my dates. I'll be glad when the time comes. The weight's slowing me down something terrible.'

She went over to the sink, filled a jug and watered the plant that stood on the windowsill above.

'That's doing well,' said Lizzie.

'Geordie took it home the day after we moved in.' Her face softened as she said her husband's name. Then, returning to her usual flippancy, she added, 'Don't know what for. It's just another thing for me to see to.'

They chatted on until Geordie came home. He went over to Agnes and put his arm round her shoulder.

'Well, you'll have enjoyed a bit of company today.'

Agnes shrugged his arm away in mock impatience. 'I suppose you'll be wanting something to eat.'

Lizzie smiled and rose to go. There were speldings to be taken in.

– 24 –

Davie

As the year wore on, the fishing went well. The women went on caring for children, cooking, and cleaning, and spending every spare moment from dawn to dusk in baiting lines. After much practice, Lizzie could now keep up with the best of them in the line-baiting.

The women would take turns at walking, in small groups, the long road to the Ythan Estuary to gather mussels. As they neared the Forvie Sands, they would hear the soft call of eider ducks and see terns hovering and diving. At the estuary, the oyster-catchers that fed on the mussels scattered as the women approached. The women's work-hardened hands were little hurt as they dug out and lifted the mussels.

But all too soon, most of the birds were flying south, before the return of winter. As the weather worsened, it was now that the women would see more of their menfolk. Janet's husband Andy, along with the two boys, were often at home. Drewie and Jamie had spent most of the past summer fishing with their father. Robbie now fished with Bill Paterson, whose own son had gone off to try his luck working in the fish market in the nearest coastal city of Aberdeen.

Andy came home late one evening accompanied by Davie Phillips. It was obvious to the two women that they had visited the Kilmarnock Hotel.

'Well, you've been long enough,' said Janet. 'Your supper will be spoiled.'

'Na, na, lass. Nothing could spoil your cooking. There's not a better cook in Collieston!'

Janet turned to the younger man, hiding a smile as she said, 'You'll stay for your supper, Davie.'

The two men sat at the table. Andy playfully spanked his wife as she leant past him to place his food on the table.

'None of that, Andy Gray,' said Janet.

He smiled foolishly, then the men bent their heads to eat.

Lizzie realised for the first time how handsome Davie was. Davie, feeling her eyes on him, looked over. Lizzie bowed her head quickly over her sewing, but not before she'd noticed the merriment in his blue eyes.

And, as time went on, despite the occasional tossing of her head and her scornful looks, she discovered that he never lost his constant good humour. Almost against her will, she found herself warming to him. One fine evening, as they sat with the family, he said, 'Time I was heading off home. Will you not walk with me to the end cottage, Lizzie?'

She looked askance at him as usual, but stood up when he did, and they strolled together to the end of the road.

'Well, goodnight then, Davie.'

As she turned to go back, she felt her face grow hot as she

heard him say, with his usual laugh, 'Well, goodnight then, Lizzie.'

Back at the cottage, Janet called Lizzie over to join her at the fireside.

'How did things go while I was away, Lizzie? Did you enjoy your time with the Patersons?'

'Oh yes. We got along well.'

'I was wondering, now that the twins are starting school, if it would be an idea for you to stay on with the Patersons. What do you think, Lizzie?'

Lizzie pondered for a moment before replying. 'That would be fine with me, but I'll have to ask Mina.'

'I'll ask her, if you like.' Lizzie nodded.

So it was arranged and, shortly after, Lizzie moved in with the Patersons.

Lizzie was feeding the baby one day when little Molly went and stood at the closed door. 'I want out,' she wailed.

'Come away here, lass, and see what your da's got,' said Bill.

With pouting lip, she went to her father. He held something in his closed hand toward her, and she pulled at his hand until he opened it. Her eyes widened, pout gone, as she saw the tiny object that lay there.

'What is it, Da?'

'It's a sea horse. You know when the waves are big and there's all white foam on them?' She nodded. 'Well, the white bits are the horses, jumping in the sea.' The child climbed onto his lap and he went on talking as the women chatted.

Mina mentioned that Agnes had visited with her baby, and what a bonny baby it was. 'And did you know that young Kirsty's expecting?'

'Kirsty?' said Lizzie. 'Oh, the poor lassie. You wonder what made her take up with a boy like Donald, a nice lass like her.'

'She was maybe looking for the kindness she never got at home,' said Mina. She went on to tell how, when Annie became aware of Kirsty's condition, she had thrown the girl out. Kirsty was now living with Donald in the run-down cottage on the hill across from the Nicols' farmhouse. Donald was taking work here and there, but even so, 'goodness knows how he can afford to drink the way he does.'

'And to make matters worse,' Mrs. Paterson continued, 'Annie and Tommy themselves have moved into another cottage house on the Thomsons' farm. There would have been room enough there for Kirsty and her baby.' She shook her head sadly, then brightened a little. 'Oh, and Annie's brother Sandy's still working at the Thomsons' farm. I hear he's a good, hard-working man.

'Well,' she said, nodding towards the two children, 'it's time we got these two ready for bed.'

– 25 –

White Horses

Though it was only midday, the sky had darkened. Mina stood at her door, listening to the boom of the sea coming from far off. She knew that one of those sudden spring squalls was brewing and, with a slow shake of her head at the thought of those still out on the sea, she went inside to join Lizzie.

Noticing the change, some of the men who had been fishing nearer the shore had already beached their boats, and others, further from the shore, were pulling hard for the little harbour.

When her husband Bill came home, Mina asked him if all of the boats were in.

'The Phillips brothers, Davie and George, they're not in yet. They went out further than the rest of us,' he said, and Lizzie closed her eyes for a moment.

Out at sea, Davie and George were fighting hard to keep themselves afloat. The swell would lift the little boat, then plunge it downwards, the spray drenching the men and blinding them for many seconds.

The seawater coming in with each swell threatened to swamp the boat as, with numbing hands, the men clung to the sides. Their catch of fish had long been washed overboard.

News of the missing brothers had spread quickly, and small groups of fishermen stood on the shore, prepared to help if help was needed. They stood silently until at last, on the crest of one of the bigger waves, the boat was thrown onto the beach. The sudden stop shot George from the boat onto the shingle and men rushed forward, some to help the brothers, others to drag the boat over the shingle and well away from the pounding surf.

Next day, the sky was clearer, but there was still enough motion in the sea to create the white-foamed waves that broke on the shingle before hissing back again. But the storm had spent itself, leaving behind some deep pools among the rocks on the shore. The women had taken advantage in the change of weather, and fish that had been split, cleaned and salted now hung from fences or lay flat on any available surface, to be dried hard by wind and sun.

Leaving the baby with Lizzie, Mina set off for Tansy's house, with Molly trotting beside her.

'We'll let Tansy see your new shawl,' Mrs. Paterson said, smiling down at her daughter, who was dressed in a smaller version of the shawl that her mother wore. Suddenly, the little girl slipped her hand from her mother's and started running down the slope that led to the rocks and the harbour. Her mother chased after her and took her hand again.

'Let me go! Let me go!' The child was looking at the still-rough sea. 'I want to see the horses!' And she struggled loose and ran on down towards the sea.

Her mother ran after her, but wasn't close enough to prevent her from tripping and falling with a splash into a deep pool. Mina let out a scream as she jumped in after her. As she sank, her frantic searching hands caught hold of the child. She was barely aware of the taste of the salt water or the fractured light as she tried to rise in the water by kicking her feet, pulled down as she was by the weight of her sodden long skirts and her boots. But the thought of her drowning daughter gave her the strength to get the child onto the flat rock above, then drag herself out. Gasping, she leant over Molly, whose eyes were closed. After what seemed like an eternity, they opened, and the little girl gave a wail, then began to sob. For the first and only time in her life, she was glad to hear her child crying.

Mrs. Greel and another neighbour had started running down the hill at the sound of the scream, and now stood above them. As Mrs. Greel lifted the still-crying child into her arms, the neighbour helped Mrs. Paterson to her feet, and they went up the hill and back home.

Later that day, Bill Paterson and his fishing partner Robbie had been out setting the lines. They had attached them to a buoy as usual, then rowed back to the shore. After hauling the boat up the shingle, they had each picked up a couple of the biggest rocks they could carry and had walked up the hill to the pool Molly had fallen into. As they dropped them into the water, one of the older men, baiting lines outside his cottage, called over.

'You fillin' in the pool, then, Bill?' Bill nodded.

By the time Bill and Robbie came up the hill with their next load of rocks, word had spread and the men of the village, who had already set their lines, came to help. It wasn't long before all the pools had been filled.

– 26 –

Harvest

The fishermen, helping with the harvest as usual, had worked hard alongside their farming friends in the hot sun. Now they were all looking forward to their break. The women brought tea in metal containers and scones spread with treacle or syrup in towel-covered baskets. Agnes came slowly across the field with little Kathy stumbling along behind her. After Geordie had eaten and drank his fill, he called his little girl over and fed her a tiny piece of scone. She took the proffered titbit, then went laughing back to her mother. 'Here's a bit more, Kathy,' he called. And so the game went on. Later, when threshing was over, the women would gather the chaff – the husks – and take them back home. There, the large hessian bags that served as mattresses would be emptied, washed and re-filled with fresh chaff.

The sweet smell from the fields drifted in through the open windows of the hall, where all were gathered for the harvest 'meal and ale' to celebrate the end of harvest. The air was filled with chatter and the occasional burst of laughter as they ate and drank. Feasting over, the floor was cleared for dancing, and this time when Davie crossed the floor to her,

Lizzie was waiting for him. They joined the same reel as Agnes and Geordie. At the end of the reel, Geordie told them he was going to the barn. He wanted to check on a cow that he thought might be about to give birth to her first calf.

The music struck up once more, and children and adults joined in a stately Strathspey. Only the youngest of the children needed help with the intricate to-ing and fro-ing of the dance. During the next break for the musicians, Lizzie stood drinking her lemonade alongside Davie with his glass of ale before he returned to pick up his fiddle again.

Some few dances later, Agnes said to Mina, 'That calf must be taking its time in coming. Geordie's been away for a while now.'

'But it's often like that with a first calving. You'll remember how long you were with Kathy.'

Agnes smiled. 'Aye, right enough.'

But soon Agnes grew restless and told Lizzie she was going out 'to see how things were going.' Lizzie said she would enjoy a bit of fresh air. Davie agreed, and the three of them left the hall and went out into the quiet night.

No sound came from the barn as Davie opened the door and went inside, followed by Agnes and then Lizzie. He had only gone a few steps when he turned and said to Lizzie, 'Get Agnes outside, Lizzie.' But Agnes struggled against Lizzie's efforts to hold her back, asking, 'What is it, Davie? What's wrong?'

Slipping out of Lizzie's grasp, she staggered forward towards the open stall. The cow stood licking its calf. Geordie lay awkwardly on the straw under the cow. For a moment, it was difficult to tell where the blood was coming from, for the afterbirth lay close to Geordie's bloodied head. Davie lifted his friend out of the stall and laid him down gently. A bucket half-full of water stood nearby and Davie dipped his cupped hand into it and cleared some of the blood away. It was then that they saw that Geordie's skull had been crushed.

'Take Agnes home, Lizzie,' said Davie.

Lizzie, her arm already round the woman's shoulders, gently turned her towards the door. With no shawls to collect on this fine night, they took the path that lead towards Drydykes. The music from the hall drifted towards them for a little time, then suddenly stopped.

Andy Gray drove his horse and cart to the front of the building, where Davie and Robbie carried the body onto the cart. Back at Drydykes, they laid Geordie on a table and covered him with a bedspread. As was the custom, curtains in the house were drawn, mirrors covered, and the clock was stopped. Four days later the funeral took place. Many of the villagers followed the coffin to the graveyard, where Alan Cowie held a short service before they returned to Drydykes.

Later, the minister was the last of the guests to leave. Lizzie walked with him to the door and went back into the farmhouse.

'I'll get the dishes done now,' she called to Agnes as she passed the room where Agnes sat. Agnes came out and followed her into the kitchen. As Lizzie washed dishes at the sink, she commented that the plant on the windowsill – the one that Geordie had taken home to Agnes – look withered, and she lifted it down.

'Och, it's time that was thrown out,' said Agnes, and she reached towards Lizzie to take it from her, but Lizzie said, 'Wait, Agnes. There's a bit of new growth there.'

Agnes looked down into the wilted plant and saw the tiny green leaves of new shoots. Lizzie now handed her the pot and Agnes, after carefully removing the dead parts and watering the plant, placed it back on the windowsill.

'Oh, why did I not let him go to the fishing?' she cried out. Then, softly, 'Oh, Geordie, my Geordie,' and she sank down on a chair and sobbed.

Just then, Kathy trotted into the kitchen. Agnes dried her eyes, held out her arms to lift her little girl onto her lap and cuddled her.

Sandy Helps Out

Mrs. Buchan had dropped in at the Thomsons' home to see Kirsty and leave her some fish, as she often did. As they chatted, Lizzie came into the kitchen.

'Well, Lizzie,' said Mrs. Buchan. 'I haven't seen you for a while.'

Lizzie smiled. 'And how are you, Mrs. Buchan, and little Daisy?'

'We're both fine. But you wouldn't know Daisy these days she's grown so much. I'm on my way to Daniel's now, to take her home. Why don't you come along and see her for yourself?'

Lizzie looked over at Kirsty.

'Aye, you go along, Lizzie. I'm finished here for now, and I'm just away home myself.'

Mrs. Buchan and Lizzie walked in the sunshine, up the hill and past the manse to Daniel's cottage. Daisy was sitting on a small stool outside. She waved and ran to them, chattering about her new wooden doll 'that Daniel made.'

'Oh, you're right, Mrs. Buchan. I'd hardly have known her.'

They had tea in Daniel's neat little house and talked until Lizzie said she ought to be going.

'Come by any time, now,' Daniel called to her as she set off.

Lizzie walked down the hill and crossed the road. Memories of her time at the manse came back to her. She remembered the day that she and Agnes had taken the children on their first picnic. Now she followed the path they had taken to the top of the hill where, as before, she admired the sweep of the sparkling sea. But as she looked down on the standing stones with their black shadows, she felt the same shiver that she'd felt the first time she'd seen them. The sound of a man's voice behind her made her jump.

'And what would you be doing away up here?'

It was Davie. As she told him where she'd been, her eyes strayed back to the stones. Davie, noticing her expression, asked what ailed her.

'You're not afraid of a few stones, surely? Come on.'

He caught her hand and, pulling Lizzie with him, ran down the hill and between the stones and their shadows, into the clearing in the middle. She turned to him, breathless and laughing, her face flushed. Some of her hair had worked loose and lay tumbled on her shoulders.

'Ah, but you're a bonny lass, Lizzie.'

He pulled her towards him and kissed her. But this time the kiss was more insistent than the kisses they'd shared until now. Lizzie resisted this closer embrace at first, then found herself responding with a warmth she had never felt before. It was easy for Davie to lay her gently on the ground. He loosened her hair till it flowed around her face and shoulders.

'Ah, my bonny lass,' he said, and Lizzie lay quiet.

That summer, with some of the villagers following the herring shoals down the east coast as usual, the visitors started to arrive. A small gathering of children stood silently watching as one family 'all the way from Aberdeen' dismounted from an open trap and entered what would be their holiday cottage.

'Can you see my da going out in the boat in them fancy clothes?' said one of the watching village boys.

'And can you see my mam baiting the lines in all that finery?' another added, sniggering.

But later, the girls from that same crowd would remember and comment on every detail of ribbon, frill and flounce.

At Drydykes farm, Agnes was dressing Kathy in her plain hand-made clothes, her mind on the forthcoming visit. She had already spoken with Mr. Nicol, the owner of Drydykes, and he had agreed that she could stay on if she could find someone to help with the heavier work. There was a knock on the door. When Agnes opened it, Annie's brother, Sandy, stood there.

'Come in, Sandy.'

With Kathy holding on to her mother's skirt, Agnes walked slowly ahead of her visitor, and into the seldom-used 'best room'. She sat down in one of the armchairs and her daughter sat on a low stool beside her. Bidding Sandy to sit down opposite them, she asked, 'You'll have spoken with Mr. Nicol, then?'

'I have that.'

'And what do you think?' Her level voice did not betray how much his answer would mean to her.

'Aye, I can come and work the land here from the Nicols' place, most days likely.'

'I think that should work out well. If you're here at midday, you'll have your meal here, of course. If you'll just let me know when you can start?'

'I could maybe start this Monday, if you're agreeable.'

'That'll be fine.'

In the next few months, Sandy worked hard and caught up with the work on both farms. For the time being, Agnes's tenancy was safe.

– 28 –

Lizzie Moves Out

Mrs. Dewar had had a restless night. Dreams of Conn had disturbed her sleep, but she was up in the early hours of the morning to bait the lines. The women sat outside, fingers busy. Tansy sat beside Mrs. Dewar, and the younger woman had been saying that 'hadn't they been lucky with the fishing that season...' when Mrs. Dewar dropped the line she was working on and stood up. Shielding her eyes against the rising sun, she looked towards the end of the row of cottages. A few moments later a tall figure appeared round the corner of the last house and came striding towards them. It was her son. When he reached her, he put his arms around her. For a moment she stood with eyes closed, then said, 'Oh, Conn! Why didn't you let me know you were coming home?'

'Well, Mother, it was kind of a last-minute decision and then there just wasn't time.'

His voice was as soft as ever, but his mother saw a hardness in his eyes that hadn't been there before.

'Come away in, then. You'll no doubt be wanting something to eat.'

Conn soon settled back into the old ways and joined Robbie and Andy as third man on the boat.

Lizzie was baiting lines while Molly amused her baby brother by dangling a piece of cloth near his face then hiding it quickly behind her back, when Mina returned from her visit to the cottage where Kirsty lived. With hardly a glance at Molly and her giggling brother, she nodded to Lizzie and went inside. Lizzie had noticed that lately she seemed to have lost her smile. Soon she returned in her working clothes, sat down beside Lizzie and picked up a line.

'Well, that's Kirsty had her baby. It was an easy birth – a boy for a change. There's been so many girls born lately.' She paused, frowning. 'And a fine father that Donald will make. Whatever's going to happen to the poor bairn?'

It was Conn who discovered, some weeks later, 'what would happen'. He had gone to visit Annie's brother Sandy. The two men got along well together, and on this fine evening they leaned on a field gate, chatting.

'You won't find me on the land – it's the sea for me,' Conn had said. Sandy was about to comment when the sound of raised voices came to them from the cottage on the hill across from where they stood. 'What's that, then?' asked Conn as he looked up towards the cottage.

'Oh, I wouldn't go interfering if I was you. That's not the first time I've heard them having a row.'

There was a scream, then another. Conn took off up the hill, heading for the cottage. As he crashed the door open, he saw Kirsty cowering and Donald looming over her, his fist raised. Conn strode in, grabbed Donald from behind and dragged him outside, as Donald shouted, 'Ger off me! Ger off!'

Donald's speech was slurred, his eyes unfocussed. He swung an awkward punch at Conn, who retaliated and caught him on the chin. Donald fell, then got up on all fours, cursing loudly.

Conn reached down and, grabbing hold of the front of his jumper, yanked him to his feet. Holding the man's face close to his own, Conn said quietly, 'Now get out. Get away from here, and if I ever see you around here again, I'll kill you.' As Donald started to argue, Conn raised his voice. 'I said get out! Now!' He watched until Donald had trudged drunkenly away towards the road before he went back into the cottage.

'Are you all right, Kirsty?' The baby was crying loudly, and Kirsty went over and picked him up, holding him close. 'It's always the baby I'm frightened for.' As she looked over at Conn, he noticed the bright red mark on her forehead.

'Would you like me to stay for a while?'

'No, I'll be all right now. He's good at hitting women, but he's a coward at heart. I heard what you said to him. He won't be back.'

Sandy still stood at the fence where Conn had left him, and from where he had watched Donald staggering off. Conn said, 'Goodnight, Sandy,' as he passed, and took the road to his home.

His mother sat with Mrs. Greel, who had just asked how little Daisy was getting along. 'The poor lass must wonder where her home is, with Mrs. Buchan or with Daniel.'

'Oh, she's doing just fine, and Mrs. Buchan and Daniel

are getting along fine together too.' Mrs. Dewar smiled. She looked up as Conn came in.

'You're early tonight, Conn. I didn't expect you for a while yet.'

'I'd better be getting home now myself,' said Mrs. Greel. 'We all need our sleep with the fishing going so well.'

And she bade them 'Goodnight.'

The following day Conn dropped by the Thomsons' to find that Kirsty was unable to get the Thomsons out of bed. At her request, he went on to Mina's to let her know that the couple had taken a bad turn and could Lizzie help out.

It was late that evening when Lizzie returned. Mina let her knitting rest on her lap as she listened to how the Thomsons seemed to have rallied again.

'Kirsty would have been glad of your help,' said Mina. 'But there's something else I need to talk to you about.'

'Aye?' asked the girl.

Mina moved nearer the fire, picked up the small iron bar and poked at the peat. 'You know, things have been different for me since the day Molly fell in the pool.' She paused, then turned round and sat down on the chair across from Lizzie. 'I was so near to losing her. Lately I think of it daily – just can't seem to shake it off. Anyway, I've spoken with Bill and he's agreed to leave the fishing and for us to move to Aberdeen.'

Two weeks later, the Patersons left, and Lizzie went to stay with Agnes.

Connon

A group of boys stood on the village street, pointing upwards and chattering excitedly. A few men straggling up from the harbour stopped beside the children and looked up, too. Janet and Nan Greel left their baiting to join them and see what the fuss was about. With a yell of triumph, the boys ran off laughing. 'The little limmers,' said Nan, shaking her head. The men walked on, smiling, as the women went back to their line-baiting.

'I hear the Thomsons took another bad turn. Funny how they seem to get ill at the same time,' said Nan.

'But neither of them ever looked that well, with their pale faces,' said Janet. 'They're lucky having Kirsty to look after them. Did you hear that Tansy's learning Kirsty to knit? You would have thought that that mother of hers would have seen to that, but I don't think that Big Annie was ever much use with the needles.'

'Aye, she's a good lass, Kirsty,' continued her neighbour. 'She's been looking after them for a while now, and her with her baby to look after as well.' Their hands worked without pause as they chatted.

'And what about Agnes?' wondered Janet. 'She's on her

own now with little Kathy. And that's a tied cottage they're in. It'll be needed by whoever comes to work the land now that poor Geordie's gone. What'll happen to Agnes and the bairn?'

'Did you not hear? Sandy's been working the land. Lizzie moved in with Agnes after Mina and her family moved to Aberdeen, so she's all right for now.'

Mr. Greel appeared at his door behind them, and the women tidied their lines to go indoors to feed their husbands.

Kirsty had brought soup and bread for the Thomsons. The young girl plumped up their pillows then emptied the pot from under their bed while they ate. As she finished she heard the sound of the baby whimpering.

'He's hungry,' said Kirsty. 'I'll just leave the dishes in the kitchen till tomorrow.' When she came back she picked up the baby, still snuggled in his blanket in the makeshift bed near the window. With an 'I'll see you tomorrow, then,' she let herself out of the farmhouse and set off for the cottage. Connon was at the door, waiting for her.

'I was at Sandy's. Thought I'd drop by with a bit of fish for you. The fishing's good just now,' he said as he followed her into the cottage.

As Kirsty prepared food for the baby, she said, 'I'll be having something to eat myself in a minute, if you want to stay.' Connon stayed.

He came quite often after that. Sometimes Tansy would be there with wool and knitting needles. One evening, when

Connon was visiting, she commented, 'You're coming on very well, Kirsty.'

'Yes, I'm beginning to feel more "at home" with the knitting as you might say. You're happy to stay with Ken, Tansy?'

Tansy smiled and nodded, and Kirsty stood up and put her knitting into its bag, saying, 'Well, the Thomsons will be expecting me about now. Do you want to come over with me, Connon? They don't get many visitors.'

As they walked, Kirsty said, 'You know, Tansy's been a real good friend to me, learning me to knit, and she often looks after Ken when I'm at the Thomsons'.'

'Aye, she's a good woman right enough, and you can see she dotes on the bairn.'

As they spoke, Tansy was sitting with the baby on her knee, talking to him softly and looking at him with adoring eyes.

One misty night Connon visited again. As was usual by now, when it came time for Kirsty to tend to the Thomsons, they walked there together.

'Kirsty, I'm thinking of moving away for a time, maybe to Aberdeen.'

There was a pause before she said, 'We'll miss you, Conn.'

He reached out and took her hand as they walked. 'If I go to Aberdeen, will you wait for me?'

They were almost at the Thomsons' door before Kirsty turned to him and said, 'Yes, Conn, I'll wait.'

– 30 –

The Will

A few weeks later, Kirsty started off on her usual morning visit to the Thomsons' house. Baby Ken had not slept well the night before, and Kirsty had been up more than once to rub his gums in an attempt to ease the teething pains. Now he slept in her arms, his head on her shoulder, as she walked slowly down the hill. Reaching the farmhouse, she pushed open the door and went along the passage and into the bedroom.

Mrs. Thomson was awake and seemed to be trying to speak. Kirsty laid her little boy gently on his bed near the window and, going over to Mrs. Thomson's bedside, took her frail hand. 'Oh Kirsty, Kirsty,' she said, and closed her eyes. Kirsty looked over at Mr. Thomson. He lay on his back, his eyes open and unblinking.

'I'll have to leave you for a minute, Mrs. Thomson, but I won't be long.' She had difficulty in pulling her hand from the old woman's grasp and turned to ask her to let go before she realised that there would be no answer. Mrs. Thomson had stopped breathing.

Kirsty was relieved when Conn offered to take over the funeral arrangements.

30. THE WILL

The news that a lawyer was coming to the Thomsons' farm to read the will soon travelled round the village. People were surprised to learn that only Annie, Annie's husband Tommy, and Kirsty would be there.

The lawyer arrived on a bright, cold Monday. Kirsty had cleaned the 'best room' in preparation for the visit. Tommy had helped pull the table and four chairs from the kitchen into the room, while Annie looked on. All three now sat at one side of the table. They had run out of what little conversation they had, and Kirsty was relieved when the door opened and the heavily-built lawyer, in his smart city clothes, came in.

'Good morning. You'll know that I'm Mr. Reynolds, lawyer to Mr. and Mrs. Thomson. I take it that you are Mr. and Mrs. Fowler, and you must be Kirsty.'

He shook each of their hands in turn, sat down across from the waiting three and put his small case on the table. Putting on a pair of half-moon spectacles, he opened the case, lifted out some documents and placed them on the table. He then leaned forward, elbows resting on the table and fingertips placed together, and looked at each of the sitters in turn.

'Now,' he said, 'I'll be reading out the will to you afterwards, but first I'll just let you know what it says in plain words. Mr. and Mrs. Thomson left everything they owned to each other. They changed their wills just lately, leaving to you, Mr. Fowler, the sum of five pounds over and above what they have already paid you, in recognition of the work that you've put into the farm these last months.' Tommy raised his eyebrows. 'And to you, Mrs. Fowler, is left the sum of ten pounds, over and above what has already been paid to you, for looking after Kirsty.'

Kirsty, frowning, looked at Annie for some explanation, but Annie was looking straight ahead. Kirsty's gaze returned to the lawyer as she heard him say, 'And to you, Kirsty, is left the farmhouse with the buildings thereon, the farm itself, and the money they have put by.' He then proceeded to read the lengthy will. 'Now, unless you have any questions, I would like to speak to Kirsty on her own.'

Annie stood up, tight-lipped, drew her shawl firmly round her ample frame and marched towards the door. Tommy, with a 'Thank you' to the lawyer and a nod to Kirsty, followed Annie out.

'Well, lass, you'll be wondering what this is all about. Mrs. Thomson wanted you to know the facts only after she had passed away. You see, Mrs. Thomson had a younger sister called Maisie who married a man called Henry Smith, and they went to live in Aberdeen. In time, they had a daughter, Christine, who also had a daughter who was born' – he paused and cleared his throat – 'out of wedlock. Christine died when the baby was born, and that baby was yourself.'

Kirsty turned her head and looked away from the lawyer. He gave her a few moments to recover before continuing.

'When Mrs. Thomson discovered that her sister Maisie wasn't well at the time, and not really fit enough to look after the new baby, she found Mrs. Annie Fowler. Mrs. Fowler had no children of her own then and was willing to look after you. She was given payment, of course. The Thomsons then moved to the farm to be nearer to you.' He took a deep breath before going on. 'So Mrs. Thomson was your grandmother's sister. Your real grandmother is Mrs. Maisie Smith, who still lives in Aberdeen. She has asked me to give you her address.' He reached across and placed an envelope on the table. 'She says she'll be glad to see you at any time.' Here he took another deep breath and leaned back in his chair. 'Now, Kirsty, the legacy and what I've just told you must have come as quite a shock. You'll need time to think it all over. Maybe you have a friend you can talk with who can give you advice?' Kirsty made no reply. She sat looking at the envelope where it lay. 'Well, whether or not, please feel free to get in touch with me if I can be of help.'

The lawyer went round to where Kirsty sat and extended his hand. She took a moment to raise her own and say 'Thank you, Mr. Reynolds,' before he left.

Oldcastle

The sun dappled the wood that the four people walked through on their way to Oldcastle. Both women were looking forward to seeing the houses that their men were building. Jane had accepted George's proposal of marriage. Lizzie and Davie would be married after their baby was born.

On leaving the wood, they took the old beaten path that would take them to the village. A small rise became a gentle downward slope, and it was George who said, 'Look! You can see the top of the old castle wall from here.' Soon they entered the village. On either side of them was a row of houses. In the middle of the left-hand row, there was a small shop.

Further ahead, as the land reached out towards the sea, houses were scattered. On a grassy hill to their right, the half-dozen women who sat baiting lines smiled and nodded to the small group as they passed and walked towards the remains of a wall that stretched above them – all that was left of the castle after which the village was named.

As they walked on, the promontory narrowed until it was just a few yards wider, on either side, than the two houses that were being built, one in front of the other. The ground at the sides fell away abruptly. Lizzie walked a little nearer to the edge and looked down on the waves that crashed onto the rocks, many feet below. She stepped back quickly and shuddered, thinking of the child she carried.

The screaming of gulls broke into her thoughts. Separated from the far end of the promontory by a narrow stretch of sea stood an enormous rock. Countless birds swooped and dived. Two or three of them winged past, and Lizzie was amazed at the brilliant colour and size of the bills on some of the small, swift birds.

Lizzie and Jane walked back to where the women sat and settled themselves on the hill. They had not long exchanged names, when there was an odd clunking sound which seemed to come from somewhere ahead and well below them. When Jane asked what it was, one of the women, Winnie by name, explained, 'Oh, that's just the "clunker". It's where we get our fresh water. The noise is the sound of someone pumping the handle.'

'It's well-named.' Lizzie laughed. 'And what about the shop we passed?'

'Mrs. Brewster runs the shop. Lost her man to the sea years ago. The shop's handy, except when the weather's really bad. That's when she can run out of things.'

A bird swooped by, and Lizzie commented on the colonies of birds on the rock.

'Oh aye. The rock's just above St. Katherine's Dub where one of the Armada ships sank.' This came from Pat. Pat was as slim as Winnie was plump, and though they both wore their hair in the usual fashion, combed back into a bun, Pat's was as fair as Winnie's was dark.

They chatted on until Davie and George joined them. The two men had finished building for the day. More stones were needed before they could continue. And so the four returned the way they had come. At the far side of the wood, they said their goodbyes. Jane and the two men took the road that turned left, she to return to Winfield, and the men to Collieston. Lizzie took the turning to the right that would take her to Drydykes.

Lizzie called out a 'Hello, Agnes' as she entered the cottage. In the kitchen, Sandy sat at the table beside Kathy. He was giving the little girl her last spoonful of food. Then, having finished his own meal, he took his leave and returned to the fields.

'He seems to have a good way with Kathy,' said Lizzie.

'Aye, he has that. Do you see the kitten there?' Lizzie followed Agnes's gaze to where a black and white kitten lay asleep in a blanket-lined basket in the corner. 'He brought it in the other night for Kathy. It's funny the way they've taken to each other, the kitten and her. She's called it Bonnie.' She got up and poured some milk into a cup and set it down for her daughter. While the little girl was busy drinking, Agnes sat down again and said softly to Lizzie, 'I think he started to say something about marriage the other day. He said "I know it's only a year..." but I said something to stop him from saying any more.'

'You still miss Geordie, Agnes.'

'I'm a lot better than I was, but everything still looks a bit, well, kind of grey, Lizzie. Folk talk to you, but there seems to

be little meaning in what they say. Little meaning in anything.'
She turned to look at Lizzie with stricken eyes. 'You know, I
never told Geordie how I felt about him.'

'Oh Agnes. Do you think he didn't know? I never saw anyone's face light up the way his did when he saw you coming.'

Agnes reached across the table and laid her hand on top of
Lizzie's.

Kathy had finished her drink, and as her mother lifted her
down, there was a rap at the door. Agnes went off to answer
it. Lizzie heard the sound of slow, heavy footsteps, and Agnes
came back into the kitchen followed by Mr. Nicol.

'Well, ladies?' he said with a smile. He was a big man, and
his florid cheeks bore witness to his life in the open air.

'Will you have a seat, Mr. Nicol,' asked Agnes, 'and maybe
a cup of tea?'

'I won't say no,' he said as he sat at the table. Agnes poured
his tea and put down a plate of her pancakes.

'Your girl's certainly coming along,' he said, nodding
towards Kathy, who stood close by her mother. 'Doesn't seem
that long since my own boys were that age.'

'And they're all doing well, Mr. Nicol?' asked Agnes.

'Oh aye, thanks be to God. They've been a good help to
me all these years. Can't vouch for young Jockie, but there's
no doubt that the other two'll be following in my footsteps.'
Having swallowed the last of his pancake, he reached for
another.

'But the fact is, it's time that Willie had a place of his own.
He's been courting for a while now. I hear that Kirsty's fallen

heir to the Thomsons' farm. Quite rightly, I think, after all she did for them. But I'm wondering what's to become of the place. Connon's courting Kirsty right enough, but I cannot see him working the farm.' He took another bite of his pancake, chewed and swallowed, before continuing. 'I'm wondering will she be selling up?'

'Well,' said Agnes, 'nothing's been said yet, as far as I know.'

'I'd better ask the lass herself. I just didn't want to intrude so soon. But then again, I have my son to think of. Well, Agnes, I enjoyed that cup of tea. You're a grand baker.'

Lizzie accompanied him to the door, where he turned and asked, 'And you're keeping well yourself, Lizzie?'

Lizzie flushed, knowing that most of the local people would have heard of her pregnancy, but she smiled and nodded. Mr. Nicol patted her arm lightly and said, 'That's fine, lass, that's fine,' before setting off down the road.

The New Arrival

Since that first visit, Lizzie and Jane had taken the walk to Oldcastle only once more, the bitter weather and Lizzie's increasing size dissuading them from going again. At Drydykes, Agnes was glad that Lizzie was there for Kathy, leaving the little girl's mother free to tend to the farm animals.

Lizzie was in the farmhouse when she went into labour in the first week of January. Agnes hurried over to Kirsty's cottage to ask her to come and help. Kirsty took Ken with her and tended to the children while Agnes stayed with Lizzie.

Davie and George were pulling the boat onto the shore at Collieston when Tansy ran down the hill to let Davie know that the baby had arrived. She invited him to come to her cottage to tidy up. George told Davie to go ahead and he'd see to the catch himself. At Tansy's house, Davie washed and changed into the clean shirt that she had made ready for him, then set off for the farm. Before he could knock, the door was opened by Kirsty.

'They're in the bedroom, Davie.'

Kirsty went ahead of him and opened the bedroom door.

She stood aside as he passed her, then closed the door and went back to join Agnes in the kitchen.

As Davie stood by the bed, Lizzie opened her eyes and smiled.

'It's a lassie, Davie.'

He took her hand before leaning over to look into the cradle.

'She's a bonnie bairn, Lizzie,' he said, 'just like her mother. Do we have a name for her?'

'I thought Margaret would suit her, after my sister and yours.' Davie nodded in agreement. 'You can pick her up if you like.'

'No, no, Lizzie. She's sleeping.' He sat on the edge of the bed, still holding Lizzie's hand. 'The house is nearly finished, so we'll be able to set a date soon. I'll just go and say cheerio to Agnes and Kirsty.' He bent over and kissed Lizzie on the forehead and left her to rest.

Lizzie was soon up and about. Though her two friends spared her the heavier work, she helped with the children and with the cooking. But it wasn't long till she felt stronger, and Kirsty could return to the farm to start cleaning the neglected house. Baby Ken was amusing himself on the floor with a few toys one day while Kirsty, with sleeves rolled up, was attempting to drag a heavy dresser from the wall when a voice said, 'That's far too heavy for you, Kirsty. Let me do it.' It was Conn. He came over and put his arms around her.

'I didn't expect to see you for a while yet, Conn.'

'So you're not pleased to see me then?'

'Oh, you know I am,' she said, 'and you couldn't have come at a better time.'

Conn released her, and they sat down together on the sofa, holding hands, as she told him the story of her inheritance. He interrupted to say with a smile, 'And here's me out in the rough seas trying to make money for us, and you a wealthy woman!'

'Mr. Nicol's made a good offer for the place, and to tell the truth I'll be glad to be rid of it.'

'So why haven't you sold it to him, Kirsty?'

She looked away as she said, 'I wanted to be here for you when you came back.'

Connon's arm went round her shoulder, and he gave her a hug.

'Will you take care of things for me, Conn – I mean speak with Mr. Nicol and arrange everything?'

'Well, now, there's a bit more to it than that. We'll need a lawyer to draw up the papers and such.'

'There's Mr. Reynolds from Aberdeen. He's the one that sorted out the Thomsons' will. He said to get in touch with him at any time.'

'That's settled then, Kirsty. I'll talk with Mr. Nicol and get in touch with Mr. Reynolds. We'll get the place sold as soon as we can.'

Home – Early Days

Lizzie and Davie were married on the twentieth of March, a Saturday. The Reverend Alan Cowie conducted the service in their new home, with George and Jane as witnesses. Just as the ceremony ended, the baby started to cry, and Lizzie took her into the bedroom to feed her.

Davie thanked the minister as he walked him towards the road. While they were gone, George and Jane slipped out, each to go to one of the two nearby cottages to tell the guests who waited there that the feasting could begin. Both Lizzie and Davie's parents, and George and Jane, would eat in Lizzie's new home, the others in two of the nearby cottages.

With the meal over, they set off to visit first one, then the other of the cottages. After spending some time in each, being toasted by friends and relatives, they returned to their own home. It was late in the afternoon when guests came, a few at a time, to give final good wishes to the newly-weds. Lizzie's and Davie's parents stayed on for the evening, until Davie's father said it was time that they were going. Lizzie's father agreed, and the two men went to hitch the pony to the little trap. When all four had settled themselves for the trip home, the young couple stood at the door and waved them off. Davie turned to Lizzie and touched the crochet collar that topped her dress. 'That's bonny,' he said.

'Tansy made it for me,' said Lizzie.

Davie put his arm round her waist, saying, 'Well, Mrs. Phillips, it's been a good day. Time we turned in,' and they went into the little cottage, closing the door on a starry sky.

Lizzie would have visitors now and then. Her father came to Oldcastle one time to deliver goods to the shop. He brought with him Lizzie's mother, and Jane and Margaret. Another day – a Sunday – Davie's parents visited them. The women of the little village dropped in now and then and, of course, Davie would be at home once the fishing lines had been set out at sea. Even so, some days could seem long for Lizzie, spending so much time indoors, often with just the baby for company.

But there came a day when the sun shone and the almost constant wind dropped. Lizzie lifted the baby from her cradle, wrapped it against her with the shawl, and stepped out of the house. Behind her, the many birds flew back and forth from the rock, calling noisily. The women, taking advantage of the better weather to bait their lines on the small hill, greeted her as she neared. Pat dropped her line and went over to pull down a corner of the shawl with her finger.

'She's fairly coming on. Margaret's a good name, Lizzie. It's my own name, you know, but I've always been called Pat,' she said, before returning to the hill and the baiting.

Lizzie continued along the path to the shop.

'Well, well, Mrs. Phillips, it's nice to see you out on such a fine day.' The little shopkeeper had already visited Lizzie at home. 'And how is she?'

'Oh, she's doing fine, Mrs. Brewster. And how are you yourself?'

'Pleased with the weather, like everybody else. It's been a long winter for all of us. Oh, we're not over the bad weather yet, but on a day like this, and with the shelves well-stocked again, I wouldn't call the queen my cousin!' she said, using one of her quaint phrases. 'Now, is there something I can get you?'

'Just a box of matches, Mrs. Brewster.'

Lizzie would have enjoyed a chat with the other wives who sat in the sunshine, but it was still too cold to keep the baby out for long. She passed them with a smile and a nod. Indoors she put the box of matches on the shelf near the fireplace, beside the one that was already there. After all, matches were always useful.

St. Olaf's Day

As the days lengthened and the winter winds dropped, there came days when Lizzie could take the baby and sit baiting for a little while with the other women. On one of these days, they were joined by Mrs. Brewster.

'Well, Lizzie, you've fairly taken to the baiting. I've tried hard enough myself, but I just never mastered it – that, or the knitting. Oh, there's someone at the shop door.' And she moved off again.

'You would think she was useless, the way she speaks,' said Pat. 'But she didn't mention her shell pictures.'

'Shell pictures?'

'Aye. She takes shells from the beach and sticks them onto wood. Makes her own fish glue to hold them, as well. There's one or two hanging on the side wall in the shop. Real nice they are.'

'I'll have to have a look next time I'm at the shop. Well, the air's cooling a bit now. I'd better take Margaret in.' She tidied away the line she had been baiting, gathered up her baby in its thick blanket and walked down past the castle wall to her home.

Early next day, Lizzie had just fed the baby and laid her to sleep in her cot when the door opened and was closed with a bang. Jane stood there, her face pale. The child had opened its eyes for a moment at the sound of the door but fell asleep again. Lizzie took her sister's hand and led her over to the wooden settle, then sat down beside her.

'What's happened, Jane? Tell me quickly.' She thought of Davie, still out at sea.

'Oh Lizzie, it's Freda. She's gone.' She put her hands over her face and started to sob.

'We'll have a cup of tea, Jane, and you can tell me the rest,' said Lizzie, giving her sister time to settle. She had stopped sobbing by the time Lizzie had set their cups of tea on the table. She sat down again beside her sister. 'Now just take your time and tell me what's happened. You said that Freda's gone. Gone where?'

'She's gone, Lizzie. She's dead.' And she told Lizzie what had happened.

To celebrate Dorothy's sixth birthday, Freda had taken her into Torry, in Aberdeen, where the townspeople were celebrating a holy day. The annual fair, dedicated to St. Olaf, had been set up in Footdee, and Freda had decided to take the ferry that would take them there, across the River Dee from Torry. Many others had made the same decision, and by the time the boat moved off, it was overloaded. A little way from the shore, a strong current had started to sweep the boat downstream. The cable that was attached to the boat and stretched to the opposite shore had snapped. The boat had tilted, then capsized.

'Some folk on the Torry side waded out to help,' Jane continued. 'One of them got hold of Dorothy and got her back to the Torry side again. But Freda's gone, and a lot of others with her, and oh, Lizzie, the poor bairn, left without her mother.' She started to cry again.

Lizzie put her arms around her sister and waited until the crying stopped before saying, 'It's a terrible thing, right enough. The Winfield folk'll help with Dorothy, but it'll hardly make up for the loss of her mother, poor lass.'

'Oh aye, they're getting together now to see who can take the bairn, and the sooner the better. Poor Matty's nearly off his head with grief.'

Just then, Davie came in. 'You'll have heard the news?'

'Jane's just been telling me about it.'

Davie sat down on the low stool by the door. 'It's a terrible thing,' he said as he pulled off his boots. Then looking over at the two women, he repeated with a slow shake of his head, 'A terrible thing.'

Jane stood up to go and Lizzie walked her to the door, then turned back to give Davie his meal.

– 35 –

A Visit from Janet

Janet held her long skirts aside, the better to step up the steep path that led from the beach to the village at Oldcastle. Nearing the top, she stopped to catch her breath and turned to look down to the sands, where Andy was helping Matty repair his boat. Refreshed, she continued up the slope to the top and along the path to Lizzie's cottage.

Lizzie was delighted to see her. She invited Janet to sit down at the fireside while she took the last tray of scones from the oven and put it on the windowsill to cool with the other trays. Then she washed her hands and hung a kettle of water on the swey to boil.

'It's good to see you, Janet. I'm getting out to bait with the other women some days, but today I just needed to get the scone bin filled again.' She sat down. 'How is everybody? Any word on how poor Matty's bearing up? And what about little Dorothy? Matty can't get out fishing and look after the bairn as well.'

'Well, Tansy's happy to look after Dorothy, except for Sundays when Matty's at home. As for Matty himself, he's thrown himself into his work, trying hard to get over his loss. He's even going out to sea in weather that nobody else will go out in. He's down on the beach now with Andy. They're having to repair the boat because he's been out when he shouldn't have been. Maybe this'll make him see sense and think of Dorothy. The poor girl's already lost her mother.'

There was a pause as each thought of the tragedy, before Lizzie said, 'And there's Kirsty as well. I was thinking about her, wondering how she's getting on.'

'Well now, it's better news there. You'll know that Kirsty's living in Aberdeen, getting a home together for when she and Conn get married and settle there. Conn'll be working for Kirsty's grandfather, and of course the grandparents couldn't be better pleased, having Ken near them. I hear they were away from home when the Thomsons died, so that's why they weren't at the funeral. And now we know why the Thomsons always wore black. You see, having no family of their own, they doted on their niece, Christine. When she died giving birth to Kirsty, they went into mourning, then they moved here to keep an eye on little Kirsty. Of course, they couldn't do much at the farm, not being farming folk... which reminds me, I hear that Conn's selling the farm for Kirsty. So they'll start married life with a bit more behind them than many folks have. Mind you, they deserve it, with Kirsty having looked after the Thomsons the way she did, and Conn's a real dependable lad.'

Lizzie piled some of the newly-baked scones onto a plate, placed it beside another plate of butter pats on the table, then poured the now-boiling water from the kettle into the teapot, as Janet continued, 'Oh, and before I forget, word has come from Aberdeen that poor Mrs. Beattie's senses are back and not only that, but the children are thriving at last. Seemingly, Mr. Beattie's got a living there, too, so it's all good news.'

As she poured their tea and sat down, Lizzie said, 'I'm glad to hear that, especially about the children. And what about your own two?'

'Drewie's seventeen already, and as tall as his father.' She smiled as she added, 'I think he's got a lass in Collieston. At least, she – that's Rona, Vi Baker's oldest – well, Rona goes all quiet and shy when Drew's around.'

'Isn't that the family that lives in one of the bigger houses, at the top of the hill?'

'Yes, that's them. Nice folk.'

'And the twins?'

'Oh, they're coming on fine, but Mrs. Gray's slowing up a bit these days. Betty's good with her, so patient, and Dorry would keep anyone from getting weary, the things she gets up to and what she comes out with!'

As they enjoyed the tea and scones, Lizzie told Janet of the friends she'd made here at Oldcastle. Soon there was a knock at the door and Andy came in. 'Well, and where's the little lass?'

Lizzie got up and went over to the cradle while Andy followed to look over her shoulder at the sleeping baby.

'It's true what I've heard then – she's a bonny lass, right enough. And you've called her Margaret?'

Lizzie nodded. 'Will you take some tea and a fresh-baked scone?'

'Now that sounds real tempting, Lizzie, but Janet will be

at me if I go and spoil my appetite and cannot eat the good supper she'll be making for me.'

'Well, Andy, you're missing a treat, I can tell you,' said Janet as she pulled on her jacket. She turned to Lizzie. 'Your scones are lovely.'

'It was good to see you, Janet,' said Lizzie. As she opened the door, there came a loud mewling sound from outside. 'You know, when I first heard that sound, I thought it was a cat.'

Andy, from behind her, gave a soft laugh. 'I think everyone must think the same until they learn to recognise the different bird calls.'

Lizzie waited until the couple had got into their trap, waved goodbye and went back inside.

– 36 –

The First Year

And Lizzie did now know the different bird calls, especially those of the seagulls. The staccato screeching as one stood with beak pointing at the sky, the soft crawk-crawk between two mating gulls, and many more. But she became accustomed to the sounds and was less aware of them as time passed. And it seemed that in no time at all, Margaret was beginning to crawl.

One warm spring morning, with only a light breeze coming in from the sea, Lizzie, looking from the window at the blue sky, said to Davie, 'It's a pity that Margaret can't be outside on a day like this, but we're too near the edge of the cliff.'

The following day, when Davie had come back from the fishing grounds and had finished his meal, he disappeared outside. Lizzie heard sounds that she couldn't identify and opened the door to see him digging not far from where she stood. On the ground nearby lay what looked like a long stone and a coil of rope. Hearing the baby whimper, she went back inside.

Davie followed her in some time later. 'That's it done then. She should be safe enough now.' Lizzie picked the baby up and went out to see the stone stake, now standing upright in the ground, just beyond the front door. She went closer to discover that one end of the rope she had seen was tied round the bottom of the stake. Davie, behind them, said, 'Once the other end of the rope's tied round her, she'll have space to crawl around, but it's not long enough for her to reach anywhere near the edge.'

Lizzie sat Margaret down and tied the end of the rope round the little one's waist, then stood back a step as Margaret toppled herself to one side and onto her hands and knees.

They watched as she crawled away, then turned to each other and smiled, just as they heard a shout. George appeared, walking towards them. 'Hi! There's a bit of fun on at Pat and Stewart's tonight. I'm away now to let the rest of them know.'

That evening Lizzie, after changing the baby and tidying herself up, carried little Margaret outside where Davie, out of habit, had been looking at the sky.

'Looks like it'll be a good day tomorrow,' he said as he slipped his arm lightly round her waist.

They heard the fiddles as they neared Pat's house, and the sound became suddenly louder when David pushed open the door.

'You're late.' Winnie laughed as she came towards them.

'Aye, it was Margaret's feeding time held us back,' said Lizzie.

'Give her to me.' Winnie opened her arms and gently took the baby from Lizzie. 'Now go and enjoy yourselves.' And, as people moved aside to let her pass, she carried the baby into the next room.

As Lizzie and Davie stood there, a young dark-haired man came towards them. 'Well, I know what Davie's tipple is. But what about yourself? We haven't met before, Lizzie. I'm Garth.'

'Oh, I'll just have some juice, Garth.'

Lizzie glanced around, enjoying the lively music and the few whirling dancers. Most of the space round the room was taken up by folks chatting and sipping their drinks.

'That's a name I haven't heard before,' said Lizzie.

'His folk named him after their farm, Garthsteen,' said Davie.

The young man made his way back to them just as the dance ended. Lizzie smiled and gave a nod of thanks as he handed her the glass.

'But what about yourself?' asked Davie.

'Oh, I've had a drink, you may be sure,' was the reply. And as the music started up again, he said, 'I think it's time for a dance now.' He grinned as he turned away and moved towards two girls who stood chatting. He held his hand out to the nearest and led her onto the dancing space.

Lizzie was enjoying herself, chatting with people she hadn't seen for a while. Janet came over, followed by Andy. Janet nodded in the direction of Conn and Kirsty.

'It's a pity they couldn't have had a proper wedding,' she said, her voice low. 'But of course with Kirsty having the baby out of wedlock...' Her voice trailed off, then picked up again. 'Still, it's good to see them wed and looking so right together.'

The rest of the evening passed happily. Mothers of the

sleeping children, including Lizzie, took turns to drop into the adjoining room to check on them. Later, Pat came over to where Lizzie stood, tapping her foot in time with the music.

'That's your Margaret wakened and having a grizzle,' she said.

Lizzie glanced at the clock on the mantelpiece. 'It's time for her feed, right enough. What do you think, Davie? Will I feed her here, or will we just go home now?'

She was pleased when he said 'home'. Good though the evening had been, she suddenly realised how tired she was.

The music faded as they walked away from the cottage under the starlit sky. Once home, Davie opened the door for her. Inside, Lizzie fed and changed her baby, got undressed and tumbled gratefully into bed.

– 37 –

A Sister

The sun sparkled on the sea behind them as Lizzie carried Margaret to the hill. Along with other wives, Pat and Winnie sat together, shelling the mussels. Pat's oldest daughter, Helen, grinned and held her arms out to take the baby. Lizzie gave a sigh as she sat down beside Winnie.

'Everything OK, Lizzie?' Pat asked, her hands still busy.

As Lizzie looked at her with troubled eyes, Pat guessed, 'It's not another bairn on the way?' Lizzie nodded.

'Well, at least wee Margaret's getting onto her feet. She'll be walking by the time this next one comes along.'

'Aye, that's true.' Lizzie nodded. 'But you'll maybe keep it to yourself for now. I haven't told Davie yet.'

She sat down, took out her knife and started the work that would go on till their next meal break.

One evening, on a day when the fishing had been good and after Davie had eaten his meal, Lizzie decided it was time to let him know of her pregnancy. They were sitting by the fire when she told him.

'I was thinking that Margaret will be well into walking, and even talking, by the time this one comes along.'

Davie gave a nod but said nothing.

The baby arrived on an October evening. Pat had been sent for and, once she had made mother and baby ready, she called Davie through. He stood by the bed, head to one side as if in question.

'Another girl, Davie,' said Lizzie. 'I haven't thought of a name for her yet.'

'Well, you could name her after yourself, Lizzie,' Davie suggested.

Lizzie smiled. 'I hadn't thought of that.'

'And she'll likely get Elizabeth,' said Pat. 'Or even Betty.'

'Yes, I like that. I like Betty,' said Lizzie, and looked towards Davie. He turned from looking at the new baby.

'Aye, that sounds fine.'

Some months later, Davie had come home from a poor day's fishing and was sitting at the open door with Betty on his knee as Lizzie hung out the washing. Margaret sat on the ground, playing happily with some stones which she was cracking together and laughing at the sound they made. Just as Lizzie stretched up to pin a jumper on the rope, Davie glanced over.

'That's not you away again!' he almost shouted. Betty began crying and Margaret ran to clutch at her mother's skirts.

Lizzie paused for a moment, then went on with the pegging. 'Well, I didn't make it by myself,' she replied.

'Maybe not, but other men have their pleasure without their wives having a bairn nigh every year!'

He stood up and carried Betty, still crying, indoors.

As the time neared for the baby to be born, Lizzie had a visit from her sister Maggie, who was now married and settled in Peterhead. Lizzie was pleased when her sister suggested that she come to Peterhead to have the baby.

Maggie had no children as yet and, as her husband worked on one of the nearby farms, she wasn't tied to the shelling and baiting. She was free to look after Lizzie's two little ones. But when Lizzie told Pat of her plans, Pat offered to take little Margaret when the time came. 'My Helen would be pleased. She's a capable lass, and she fairly dotes on your Margaret.'

And so it was that Davie drove Lizzie and Betty in the cart to Peterhead, ahead of the date that the new baby was expected to arrive. It was on a coolish autumn day, with the haar coming in from the sea making it difficult to see ahead at times. By the time they had reached Maggie's house in Peterhead, the horse had cast a shoe. Davie hurriedly dropped them off. He would have to get the horse shod locally before taking the road home again.

One evening a few days later, there was a knock at the door. Davie left his meal on the table and went and opened it. Pat stood there.

'There's news from Peterhead, Davie. The baby's come a bit early, but they're both fine.' She paused for a moment. 'It's a boy.'

Davie thanked her and closed the door. Pat was surprised at his lack of response, but as she walked away she heard the sound of a fiddle. Davie was playing a happy Scottish reel.

– 38 –

Celebration

Following the spirited reply that Lizzie had made to him when she fell pregnant for the third time, Davie had little or no comment to make when Lizzie went on to bear four more children in the following six years.

One day, when the older children were at school, and the two youngest played with crab shells nearby, Pat said, 'Have you heard about Carrie and Willie Black?'

Lizzie stopped shelling, shaded her eyes from the sun and asked, 'Heard what?'

'Seems they've had enough of the new country and they're coming home.'

'Well, it took them long enough to get fed up with it. How long have they been away for? It must be ten or twelve years.'

'Aye, it would be about twelve years anyway. The oldest of their two children would be about twelve now.'

Just then, she heard the voices of the rest of her family as they appeared on the path behind them. They had walked home from school as usual.

As she stood and smoothed down her skirt, she said, 'I wonder if Carrie and Willie will be home in time for the wedding?' Pat's daughter Helen was to wed Garth.

'No idea,' Pat responded. 'But it would be nice if they were. I just hope that the storms we've had this last while will lighten up a bit. If they don't, it'll be enough to send them back again.'

Carrie and Willie were home in time for the wedding. After the ceremony, just as it began to rain, everyone gathered in the big netting shed, made ready for the celebration. Feasting over, the tables were cleared, chairs set round the edges of the hall, and the musicians struck up the first notes of a reel. As everyone found a seat, Lizzie heard a voice behind her.

'I'll sit with you, Lizzie.' It was Carrie. 'There'll be more time for a chat than there was earlier.'

They sat down together.

'Well, for one thing, Carrie, I did wonder what brought you home after all this time.'

'It's the word you just used – "home". You see, when we first went out there, there was so much to settling in. Getting to know the people and everything else that goes with a new country. A lot of the folk there had come over from the Highlands and had stayed. So we felt quite at home for a while. Willie took work at the whaling, then of course I had Evelyn not long after we arrived. So, what with one thing and another, we were kept pretty busy. Evelyn was just a toddler when Alison arrived, and the time just seemed to fly.' She paused for a moment. 'That is, until just lately. I don't know, Lizzie, but I just started to miss so many things.' She smiled. 'Funnily enough, what really decided me in the end was when a couple of lads came over from not far from here, and when I heard that familiar tongue, the longing for home just got too much for me. And what about yourself, Lizzie?'

'Well, you'll have heard that we've got seven children now. It's a big family, I know, but now that they're here, I couldn't imagine being without any of them,' said Lizzie. 'It's been hard at times, especially these last few years. There's been a lot of bad storms, and the weather doesn't seem to be easing up at all.'

Later, Lizzie noticed Winnie coming towards them. 'Looks like it's my turn to be with the children,' said Lizzie.

'Will I come with you? It'll be a chance to get to know them.'

They crossed the hall and entered the room where the younger children were being looked after. Among the half-dozen were Lizzie's Marion and Billy.

'Our turn now, Sally,' said Lizzie as she lifted a baby from the woman who had been caring for the children, helped by Winnie.

Billy smiled to his mother from the upturned chair in which he sat, making clicking noises to the imaginary horse that pulled his imaginary cart, while from Marion came the words 'No, it's my baby.'

As Lizzie went over to the two girls who were pulling at a doll, she heard the rain on the window.

'Hope that's off by the time we're all ready to go home,' she said to Carrie. Then, to the children, 'Time to lie down now.'

After Lizzie had tucked two of the children into the single bed, Billy and Marion took great delight in snuggling down under blankets on a mattress on the floor. Carrie had put the other two little boys – brothers – into a similar makeshift bed. The children settled well, and the two women were able to sit and chat softly.

Later, when another two women came to relieve them, Lizzie and Carrie were able to return to the festivities. But Lizzie's hopes for a change in the weather were not to be realised. By the time everyone left, it was raining heavily.

– 39 –

The Great Storm

Lizzie gave a last pump of water from the clunker, filling the second pail, then started slowly up the hill. The breeze which had blown in from the sea for most of the day had gone, and there was a strange stillness now. As she reached the house, she looked up at the sky. Even in the short time that it had taken to fill the pails, the sky had darkened. Now there came a rumble of thunder. At the door, Lizzie put down one pail and lifted the latch with her free hand then, picking up the pail again, went into the house. Maggie came forward and shut the door behind her.

'The sky's looking real dark now, Mam,' she said.

'Aye,' her mother responded. 'We'll have to light the lamps early again.' She carried the pails into the kitchen, passing three of the younger children as they enjoyed a bit of squabbling at the smaller table. There came a loud rumble of thunder. The children stopped their chatter and started to count towards the expected flash of lightning and gave a cheer when they saw the flicker of light through the closed window shutters. They could hear the wind rising, until suddenly it became a scream. Maggie, seeing the fear on little Ellen's face, put an arm round her and held her tight for a moment.

Later, as the wind continued to howl and scream round the house, Lizzie decided they'd all go to bed as usual.

'Shouldn't think there'll be much sleep for us tonight,' she said, 'but at least we can rest.'

After one of the girls' beds had been pulled into the larger bedroom, they all lay down, Lizzie sharing her bed with the two youngest, while Maggie, Betty and Ellen shared another. John affected a relaxed demeanour – he was a man after all. Taking little William's hand, he led him into the small bedroom, where he pulled off his own boots, then his brother's, and threw them across the floor. Without bothering to undress either himself or William, he bundled the little boy under the bedclothes then quickly followed him and pulled the bedclothes over their heads.

As Lizzie had predicted, there was little sleep for anybody that night for the noise of the wind and the rattling of the shutters. But the shutters stood firm.

Thank God Davie can be trusted as a carpenter, thought Lizzie, then she tried not to think of him or where he and his brother might be now.

She dozed off but awoke with a start. It took her a moment or two to think what was different. The screaming of the wind had stopped and, though the shutters were still rattling a little, the sudden calmness felt uncanny.

Still fully dressed, she eased herself away from the bed and walked quietly across the room, opened the door and stepped outside into the morning light. Avoiding the debris of broken pieces of wood, dead seabirds and the many stones that lay scattered around, she moved slowly to the edge of the promontory and looked down. At the place where the boats had been pulled up, well above the rocks and the high tide, all that was left of the boats were a few broken pieces of wood.

After breakfast, Lizzie and the older children spent some time clearing the space around the outside of the house as best they could.

'There'll be no lack of kindling for the fire now!' John said. No-one responded to his attempt at humour.

Back indoors, it was late in the afternoon when Lizzie stood up slowly from where she had been sitting.

'What is it, Mam?' asked Marion.

But their mother made no reply as she walked to the door. As she opened it, the children crowded round the door then moved back again as Davie, shouting a goodbye to someone behind him, came in. Lizzie walked back to the fireplace and lifted the pot from the swey as the others started chattering.

'You're safe, Dad!'

'What happened?'

'We were thinking you were lost.' This from Billy.

Lizzie interrupted the chatter with, 'I'll put some hot water in the basin in the bedroom if you want to wash.'

Later, when they had all eaten, Davie told his story. Garth had now joined the brothers in their boat, and at sea they had noticed the darkening clouds and the strange silence and had headed for the shore.

'It was just as well we were so near Peterhead, for we'd not long got ashore and into Maggie's house when it started. We were luckier than some. There's more than one woman's lost a husband or son.'

News of those drownings reached them over the next few days. Also over the next few days, they spoke with neighbours who had decided to move to Aberdeen to live there permanently. After some time of storms and the resultant poor fishing, the violent storm had been the last straw for them. Lizzie would fain have left too, but she was wise enough to hold her peace, knowing that, as head of the household, it would have to be Davie's decision.

It was two days later, while their older offspring washed clothes in the outhouse and the younger ones played outside, that Davie came over and sat across the fireplace from Lizzie. She looked down at her knitting as he spoke.

'Well, it's been some winter, lass,' he said, using a word she hadn't heard in a long time.

'Aye, Davie, it has.'

'There's as many local folk left for Aberdeen, they're being called "the trekkers".' He paused for a moment. 'I'm thinking it's time we thought about joining them.'

'Well, if you say so, Davie.' She kept her eyes on her knitting. 'When would we start?'

'There's nothing to stop us getting ready today. I've been talking with the other men and there's a few folk leaving tomorrow, if you think we'll manage to join them.'

'Yes, we should manage that. We can start getting ready tonight.'

– 40 –

Leaving

Lizzie knew by the slant of the sun at the window that it was time to get up. *Get up and get out*, she thought. After dressing, she stoked the fire, hung the pot of oats and water on the swey and went over to waken the children.

She shook Maggie by the shoulder, who slowly opened her eyes.

'What time is it, Mam?'

'Time you were up and getting ready for Aberdeen.'

The girl was wide awake now. The adventure was about to begin. They were going to the big city. Lizzie wakened the rest of the children. She changed little Jane's nappy and dressed her while the others got dressed, the older ones helping the younger ones.

Breakfast over, Lizzie and Davie took one of the chaff mattresses out to the cart where the backboard was let down and laid the mattress on the bottom. The rest of the family followed, with the three older ones carrying another of the light-weight mattresses. As Davie and Lizzie placed it on top of the first and covered it with a tarpaulin, there was a bit of jostling and bickering between the children. This stopped when they heard Davie's firm 'Behave yourselves.'

As Davie checked the horse's harness, Lizzie disappeared into the house and re-appeared with a cardboard box. It contained one or two mementoes that were precious to her. Moving one of the children a little, she placed it in the far corner of the cart.

There was much to-ing and fro-ing from houses to carts that morning. The voices of adults and excited children mingled with the jingling of harnesses as the last of the fisher-folk of Oldcastle prepared to leave.

Around midday they started to pull out, with Pat and Arthur's horse and cart leading the way. As the cart carrying Lizzie and her family passed the empty shop, Lizzie thought of Mrs. Brewster. She had left the week before with Sandy, along with Mrs. Buchan and Daisy, and old Mrs. Robertson.

And so the carts moved slowly on and out of Oldcastle, carrying the families towards new lives. Behind them the village lay without sound of human voice. Only the seagulls, free to scavenge, screamed as they dived, before flying out again over the sea.

Printed in Great Britain
by Amazon

36045170R00098